The
Spying Game

The Spying Game

Pat Moon

G. P. Putnam's Sons
New York

First American edition, published in 1999 by G. P. Putnam's Sons,
a division of Penguin Putnam Books for Young Readers,
345 Hudson Street, New York, NY 10014.
G.P. Putnam's Sons, Reg. U.S. Pat. & Tm. Off.
Originally published in 1993 by Orchard Books, London.
Published simultaneously in Canada.
Printed in the United States of America
Designed by Tony Sahara. Text set in Giovanni.

Library of Congress Cataloging-in-Publication Data
Moon, Pat. The spying game / Pat Moon.—1st American ed.   p.   cm.
Summary: After his father is killed in a traffic accident,
twelve-year-old Joe Harris becomes obsesssed with punishing the
man he thinks is responsible, but his plan gets out of control
when he discovers that the man's son is a classmate.
[1. Death—Fiction. 2. Grief—Fiction. 3. Revenge—Fiction.
4. Fathers and sons—Fiction.] I. Title. PZ7.M777Sp   1999
[Fic]—dc21   98-13069   CIP   AC   ISBN 0-399-23354-7
10   9   8   7   6   5   4   3   2   1
First Impression

Thanks to Sam
for the low-down on life as a paperboy
and to Ben
for letting me read his diary

The
Spying Game

Chapter 1

I'm crossing the car park when I see the man who killed my dad. He's pushing a trolley loaded with plastic garden chairs.

I can't believe it. I wait behind a white van and watch. What right has he to be acting normal? I mean, it's not even as if you *need* garden chairs, is it? It's not *urgent*, like a leaking roof or something. How could he even be thinking of sitting out in the garden, just months after murdering someone?

There's a boy with him: big, older than me, I'd say, fourteen or more. He's wandered off now and the man is shouting at him to come and help and the boy is ambling back slowly, hands in pockets, moody, kicking a stone.

And I remember all those times, like when I was too young to be left at home on my own, and Mum and Dad would drag me around the do-it-yourself

1

shelves, discussing endlessly whether to have the green or pink tiles and comparing the shower curtains, and every time I asked how much longer, they'd always say, "Just a few more minutes, Joe." But it never was. It was always a lifetime.

Yet I'd give anything now to get those times back, to be trailing after Dad, only I wouldn't whine this time. I'd be watching Dad and holding his hand, and helping.

The man and the boy have finished loading now. And suddenly I feel angry and I hate that kid, because he's got his dad; and he doesn't even look pleased about it.

As I watch them drive off, I notice a sticker in the back window. It says, WE'VE SEEN THE LIONS OF LONGLEAT.

I head for the door. Don't think I'm here by choice: Mum sent me. There's this roll of wallpaper on order that they've been keeping, and they keep ringing to say it's ready for collection. This wallpaper goes back to B.T.A., which is short for what Lucy calls Before The Accident. But that's like another place.

It's Saturday and there's a long line and when I get to the front I'm in the wrong place anyway, but at last I get the roll of paper. I stick it under my arm and hope I don't meet anyone I know. It's all pink roses and flut-

2

tering butterflies; even Dad didn't like it, but Mum insisted. I wonder whether it will ever get pasted up. Dad used to do all of that. And suddenly it hits me that Dad might be alive now if it wasn't for this wallpaper or if he'd bought enough rolls in the first place. So, if he hadn't run out of paper that Sunday, just before he reached the bathroom door, things would have been different. "Just popping along to B&Q to get another roll," he shouts, and Mum answers, "Well, be quick because dinner's nearly ready." And we never see him again. All for a roll of stupid wallpaper.

Then I get to thinking that his last words before that lunatic forced my dad off the road were probably something really meaningless, like "Could I order a roll of Olde English Rose Garden, please?" Or if Mum had measured up properly in the first place, or if she hadn't chosen a wallpaper that they'd run out of, and then I start thinking that perhaps it's all her fault. Then I think, maybe, if I hadn't . . .

But I stop there, because I'm home now and I don't want to think about it anymore.

"You took long enough," says Mum, picking up her bag and grabbing a list.

No "Thanks, Joe" or anything, and she doesn't even look at the wallpaper.

"Right, I'm off to get some shopping. Tom's in the garden with Matthew, so keep an eye on them."

I try to tell her that I have plans to call on Simon to see his new disk, but she's not listening.

"And tell Lucy when she eventually decides to get up to go and ask about that Saturday job in the Co-op," and she's gone.

Through the window I can see Tom with his friend Matthew. They're both wearing camouflage outfits with matching helmets. I used to say things about Tom like "I'm a very patient person. To prove it, my brother is still alive." But I don't say it anymore; it doesn't seem so funny.

But he's a real pain at times, and lately he's been a chronic ache.

The youngest definitely gets it easier. All my old toys for a start: my Action Man tank, my Lego space station, my space hopper, my Superman outfit. But does he look after it all? He's already broken two of the hippos on my old Hungry Hippos game, and I had that for years.

I wander out, down the path. Tom's crouching behind a bush, aiming a gun at the shed. But when I look closer I see it's my old space gun with the three different sound effects that I saved up for months to buy; something I definitely did *not* give him, which I keep in the top of my cupboard.

"Oi!" I say, grabbing it. "Who said you could go into my room and help yourself?"

And then Matthew's charging out from behind the shed with *my* jet-power water pistol, yelling, "Got you covered—I win!"

"No, you don't!" shouts Tom, leaping up. "You'd never have found me if Joe hadn't given me away. I hate you!" he says, turning to me. "You spoiled our game. It took me hours crawling on my stomach behind the flowers. I hate you!"

"Serve you right," I say, "for pinching things that don't belong to you. And don't go in my room without my permission. Got it?"

"I'm not playing anymore!" he yells, and runs indoors.

Matthew looks at me like I'm one of the ugly sisters and Tom is Cinderella or something and follows him indoors, and I can't be bothered to get my water pistol back.

"What have you done now?" complains my sister Lucy, who has at last crawled out of her bed and is in the kitchen making one of her weird potions with muesli and chocolate spread and honey and stuff. She looks like something from a horror comic with her long black hair hanging over her face and pale, thin legs protruding from a huge baggy T-shirt.

"Better keep out of the daylight in case you crumble into dust," I say, quite impressed with my own wit.

But she just makes a face. At least, I think she does. I can't see all of it, only her mouth, which goes into a sort of snarl.

I remember Mum's message.

"Mum says don't forget about—"

"—the job at the Co-op," she says in a singsong voice. "Doesn't she realize I need some rest? GCSEs aren't like the exams she took, you know. And has she seen the Co-op uniform? I mean, she's got to be kidding."

She takes her horrible concoction into the sitting room, slamming the door behind her, and I hear the TV switch on.

Then, suddenly, Matthew shoots across from the hall, chased by Tom, who now has the water pistol, and they disappear into the garden.

Upstairs, in my room, I set to disguising the graffiti on my bedroom wallpaper. My walls are a constant cause of embarrassment to me and abuse from my friends. It was the one time in my life I was given a say in the choice of wallpaper, and I mucked it up. True, I was only four at the time, and at four you can't imagine ever being twelve, or that one day you might actually go off the Mister Men. I've done my best to cover it with posters and stuff, but there are an awful lot of Mr. Grumpy and Mr. Muddles still peeping out.

Dad's been promising—sorry, correction. Dad had promised for yonks that he'd do my room next, but Mum had been going on about the bathroom. If only he'd kept his promise, then he might still be here, mightn't he? Okay. They might still have been one roll short when he eventually got round to the bathroom, but it wouldn't have been at that particular moment, on that particular Sunday, when that particular idiot who had seen the lions of Longleat Safari Park was driving along that particular bit of road at that particular time. Which leads me to thinking, there are so many *if*s that perhaps it was meant to happen: perhaps there is such a thing as fate; perhaps it had all been planned out on some great chart somewhere.

But then my thoughts go back full circle. It must have been *someone's* fault: Mum's or Dad's even. But that only makes me start to feel angry; that they let it happen. Or was it my fault? The thoughts go round and round like a top till my head's spinning, till I'm

7

thinking, This is stupid. There's only one person to blame for this, and that's Longleat Man.

I'm thinking all of this while I'm drawing a pair of boxer shorts on Mr.Topsy Turvy with a black felt tip. I won't go into details, but my friend Richard got a bit carried away with his pen last night and drew something quite rude. I've got a feeling Mum would not like it if she saw it. Though I doubt somehow that she'd notice; there are quite a lot of things she doesn't notice lately. My pen goes through the wallpaper and a little triangle peels back. What a mess. I throw my pen across the room.

Someone's drawn a spider hanging by a thread from Mr. Nosey's nose and there are speech bubbles all over the place. Nothing very witty, though: stuff like "Down with school" or "I vote Conservative," and some clever clogs has given Mr. Silly fangs and a black cape.

All at once, I'm in B.T.A. time again and I'm looking up, watching Dad on the stepladder, stretching up with a strip of wallpaper and it's all folded up like a concertina. He's lining it up at the top, then unfolding it against the wall, and turning to me and saying, "Hand me that brush, Joe." As he smooths out all the bubbles and creases, he's saying, "Nearly finished— you'll be able to move back in tonight." And I swear I can smell that wet-paper-paste smell. I decide I don't care what anyone else thinks; I'm keeping this wallpaper, and if Richard or Simon or anyone doodles on it again, they're going to get it, from me, personally.

Then two things happen. First there's a great wailing sound from downstairs and I'm about to leap into action and go to investigate when I hear the front door slam. I'm halfway down the stairs when I see that the horrible noise is coming from Tom, who's standing in the hall holding out his hand, and there's Mum bending down looking at it, surrounded by her shopping bags, all spilling out, and then she's looking up at me and shouting, "I thought I told you to keep an eye on him—can't you do anything I ask?" At which point Tom howls even louder and I know there's no point in saying anything.

"It hurts!" he's yelling. "It hurts!"

It turns out he's got a splinter that you'd need a telescope to see, it's so tiny.

"Fetch me a needle and some antiseptic," orders Mum.

I go to Mum's needlework box in the sitting room. Lucy's left the TV talking to itself. The curtains are drawn and her dish of horrible food is uneaten on the coffee table with the spoon resting in a blob of it on the table. But it's not my problem. I fetch the antiseptic from the bathroom and try to ignore the long dingy strip of gray wall where the paper ran out.

I'm just making myself a cup of coffee—Tom has miraculously recovered and he and Matthew are taking it in turns to shoot ants with the water pistol—when Mum comes in, full steam, clutching Lucy's dish and mucky spoon.

"I've just about had it up to here!" she's yelling as if it's my fault. "Do I have to come home to this?"

I won't bore you with the rest; you've probably got the idea. She doesn't even notice that I've left. I can still hear her, crashing about downstairs.

I'm sitting on the steps by the Haymarket, in Norwich. This is where I sometimes meet up with Richard and the rest on a Saturday, but there's no sign of them. I'm not sure I'm in the mood, to tell the truth.

There's a crowd watching a robotic dancer performing, just in front of Littlewoods. He's really good. I wish I could do that sort of stuff. He's dressed all in white with a white plastic face and helmet; he must be really hot in there. It must be great to be able to do something that makes people want to watch you or clap or laugh. Lucy can: she plays the clarinet. She's really good: won all sorts of prizes and certificates. I'm quite good at maths, and geography, but it's not the sort of thing that makes people cheer or give a round of applause, is it?

The robot has finished now. He's packing up and a man with a guitar is waiting to take his place when I see Richard and Simon coming out of the sports shop, and suddenly I don't want to see anyone, not even Richard, so I slip away before they see me.

I make my way through the outdoor market. I bet I could find my way round here wearing a blindfold, just using my nose. First thing that hits me is the stench from the fish stall, enough to put you off your fish fingers sometimes. Then as I nudge my way along there's this delicious smell of strawberries from the stalls at the front. As you turn up toward the middle you get layers of smells. You can almost eat them: cheeses, pies, bread, coffee, and there's a certain spot where it all mingles together. But the best is the crisp, hot-fat smell of chips that's getting to me right this minute, and by now I'm really hungry and trying to decide if I've got enough for a small bag of chips. I'm searching in my pockets, when I see Dad. Just his head and shoulders, his back to me, way down the slope, by the Tool Box, his favorite stall. He's wearing his denim shirt, the one with the frayed collar. And I don't care about the chips and I'm running down toward him, but it's too crowded and I knock against this old lady with a basket on wheels and she's shouting something after me, but I don't care.

I know it can't be Dad, not really, but a stupid thought comes to me as I try to get round a baby buggy that's blocking my way, that perhaps it was a big mistake, that it wasn't really Dad in the car, that somehow he'd got out and walked away, perhaps lost his memory, that he'd given a lift to someone, and that's who they found in the car with his face smashed in. I've got it all worked out: it's just a case of mistaken identity.

But when I get there and stare up at him, he's not a bit like Dad. And I'm standing there out of breath, staring up at this stranger who's looking at me as if I'm a nutter. I pretend to be looking at the wire cutters when the lady on the stall says, "Oh, it's you, love. Did your dad like the screwdriver, then?" She remembers me, see. I come here for Dad's present every Christmas and birthday, because that's what he liked best, a new tool or something. I got him the screwdriver for his birthday back in February, which seems like another life, although it's only four months ago. So I say, "No. He's dead." And I can see she's a bit lost for words and all she can manage is, "Oh—I'm sorry," and I wish I hadn't said anything, because she's really quite nice and now she looks embarrassed.

He never got his screwdriver. His birthday was four days after the accident. A complete waste of money.

I buy myself some chips, though I'm not really hungry now, and go to sit at the top, by the war memorial. It's not too savory round here; you have to be careful where you sit sometimes. A boy in a leather jacket with the sleeves torn off is stretched out on one of the seats, facedown, so I avoid him and sit next to an old lady feeding the pigeons. She doesn't look the sort who's suddenly about to throw up on my trainers or threaten me with a fist. But you can't be too sure; I suppose even hooligans grow into old people.

I'm just tossing my last chip to a pigeon with only one foot when I see the Lions of Longleat Man again. Only, this time, he's with a woman. Twice in one day; it's got to mean something.

Before I have time to think, I'm following them. He's going thin on top and he's tried to cover it up with a part that's practically down to his ear. I hate that. Dad had really thick hair.

They stop to look in a travel agent's window and, smoothly, I wander past on to the sports shop and pretend to study the display of tennis rackets. The more I watch him, the more I hate him. The way his T-shirt is too tight and the horrible reddish fluff on his arms.

I can hear the woman say, "I quite fancy Portugal," and I feel like shouting, "Well, I'd quite fancy having my dad alive, only your husband killed him!"

Brittany: that's where we were going. All booked and everything. It was great, the same place we went last year, even the same camper. You know, one that's all ready waiting for you, fridge, cooker, everything. Mum had to cancel it. Said we couldn't afford it now.

And yet here's Longleat Man, walking about, driving his car, free as you please. It would have been different if it had been a gun or something. They'd probably have locked him away. But a car's a weapon, isn't it? If it kills someone? Mum says it could still be months before the case gets to court, and all the time he's getting away with it. It's not right; not right that he should be buying garden chairs and choosing holidays, not when he killed Dad.

I almost don't notice that they've moved on, and have to walk fast to catch up. Past the bus station, then toward Sainsbury's, and this is where it starts to get difficult, because it's clear they're going in. First I think I'll wait outside till they come out, then I realize it's got all these doors, so I have to follow them in. I'm beginning to feel old. First, a morning in B&Q and now the supermarket. Is this what the future holds? It's too depressing to think about.

It's a relief when all they buy is some bottles and a few cans of drink, but my heart sinks when they head for the coffee shop. By the time they come out I'm an expert on How to Cope with Holiday Tummy and Strawberry Treats for the Family, having studied most of the newspapers and magazines on the newsstands. They don't even give me a second glance as I follow them through the automatic doors, though the girl on the cash register is giving me a funny look.

Not that Longleat Man would recognize me, though I know him all right. Not from the inquest. Gran wouldn't let me go to that, said there was no point. But I needed to know, didn't I? He was my dad. I had to know what happened. I didn't even get to see him. And I can't help wondering why. What was so dreadful that I shouldn't see? It makes me imagine some pretty awful things. All I know is what I read in the *Evening News* at Richard's: *Mr. Peter Harris was taken to the Norfolk and Norwich Hospital, where he died shortly afterward from his injuries. Mr. Harris's family did not wish to talk about the tragedy today. Mr. Terence Moss, the driver of the other car, was uninjured. Anyone who saw the accident or who may have information is asked to ring the police on Norwich . . .* I remember every word.

No. It was at the police station I saw Longleat Man. I'd gone with Mum a few days after to pick up Dad's stuff from the car. They take everything out, see, so they can check the car over for faults and stuff. There it all was: his wonky sunglasses, a half-eaten packet of mints, his maps, the little tin he kept full of change for parking, my *White Dwarf* magazine I'd left on the backseat, his bag of tools, an oily rag even, and one of Tom's pocket-monster figures that he lost ages ago. I was blinking like mad to keep the tears back and swallowing so hard it hurt, so I pretended to need the loo and shot off down the corridor, leaving Mum signing for it all.

I was just coming out when a door opens and there's a policeman and another man and he's saying to him, "Well, thank you for your help, Mr. Moss. We'll be in touch. Your car is ready for you at the back."

I know that name. He's the driver of the other car. I read it in the paper: Mr. Terence Moss.

I'm so wrapped up in my thoughts that I've almost forgotten what I'm doing and they're way ahead. I can't believe how far we've come. Then I realize we're here: this is where they live. There's his red Escort with its Lions of Longleat sticker, parked in the drive.

I overtake them just as they slip into the front door

and disappear inside. They haven't even noticed me, and I feel really good. I make a mental note of the house number and stroll on: 36 Abigail Road. I can't stop thinking about it now, about Longleat Man—how he's to blame for it all. But I'm feeling really chuffed that I followed them; that they haven't even noticed. I've got one up on him. By the time I get home, I know what I'm going to do.

Chapter 2

I need something to write it all down in: a proper notebook, not scraps of paper. It's got to be done properly. I remember the big desk diary that Aunt Beryl sent me at Christmas; she always wins first prize for the most boring present. It's probably under my bed somewhere.

A collection of dusty socks, a 1996 *Beano* calendar, a Mother's Day card that I made years ago and which never reached its destination, and, loads of junk later, my fingers make contact with something I can't quite make out. I tug it free. It's Dad's birthday present: the one he never got. You'd never guess it was a screwdriver, though, not the way I've padded it round and round with thick layers of newspaper to keep him guessing.

I don't know how long I've been sitting here on the floor with the parcel on my lap. I don't remember picking off the little bits of paper that are now all over the carpet. All I know is, I'm feeling pretty stupid with tears rolling down my face and my nose running and my mouth slobbering, like I'm a baby. I'm trying hard not to howl, real loud, choking it all back, checking the door's shut and no one can hear. I'm not a kid; I'd hate it if anyone walked in and saw me like this. Well embarrassing.

I shove the parcel back under the bed and, checking there's no one about, nip into the bathroom to splash my face with cold water. I suck up some water from the tap, tip my head back, and gargle. My throat feels like I've swallowed a small hedgehog. I look in the mirror. I'm a mess: my eyes are all red and puffy. They're brown really, what you can see of them, like Mum's, though I haven't got dark hair like her or fair hair like Dad and Tom. Mine's a sort of in-between brown. I'm an in-between sort of person, really: no distinguishing features at all. We had to do this thing in English once, describing each other and then the rest of the class having to guess who it was. Some were dead easy. Everyone knew straightaway that a red-haired stick insect with glasses and freckles was Simon. Jonathan, who was trying to describe me, said he never realized how boring I was. I was probably the most average person he knew. Then he remembered that I can touch my nose with the tip of my tongue, but no one else knew that, so it didn't help much. Last term even, when we had a student teacher, he called me John for six whole weeks. I gave up trying to tell him.

It's just as well, really. I don't want to stand out in a crowd. For what I'm going to do, I need to merge into the background: I'm going to become the invisible boy.

The diary, it turns out, is stuck between my bed and the wall. I also discover the pajama bottoms that I thought I'd left behind on the school field-study trip to Derbyshire. Mum'll be pleased, I think. She's only just bought me a new pair.

I can't remember writing anything in it, but it seems I did, for thirteen whole days. At the front it says IN CASE OF ACCIDENT PLEASE INFORM, and I've written, ME. I want to be the first to know.

Ha, ha. I can't believe that all I wrote in it for Christmas Day was "Got this diary." What about my computer, my best present ever?

It's full of other exciting information, like, "Got up. Richard came round," "Back to school unfortunately," "Think I've got a wart," "Norwich 2, Aston Villa 1," "School totally and utterly boring—French AND Mr. Liversage." Then there's a huge gap till 17th February when it says, "Remember I've got this diary." And that's mostly it, except for 15th November where it says MY BIRTHDAY in big purple capitals.

It's weird lying here on my bed, flicking over the pages for January. The person who wrote this was someone else, not me. The person who wrote, "Felt sick in Maths." didn't have a clue, did he, about what was coming? If only I could turn the days back, like the pages, everything could be okay again. Each time I'd get to Saturday, 22nd February, I could start again with Christmas Day. I wouldn't care about my presents and it wouldn't matter how many times I felt sick, or how boring school was, or if I was covered in warts, it would still be better, wouldn't it?

I turn the pages till I reach The Day: Sunday, February. It looks so clean and ordinary: no warning signs, no flashing lights, no bloodstains. Just SUNDAY, 23RD FEBRUARY, Week 8. I used to think it'd be great to have magic powers, like being able to see into the future and stuff, but I can see now it's not such a good idea. Ace for predicting football scores and winning the lottery or something, but not if it meant knowing that on 23rd February your dad was going to get smashed into a telegraph pole.

I pick up my black felt tip but change my mind

and search round for a red one. It's more of a pink really, but it'll do. Under SUNDAY, 23RD FEBRUARY I write:

ON THIS DAY MY FATHER WAS KILLED
BY A LUNATIC WHO SHOULD BE
LOCKED AWAY FOR EVER AND NEVER
BE ALLOWED ON THE ROADS AGAIN.

I study it for a few minutes. Then I turn the pages till I get to Saturday, 27th June: today. I start to write, making my writing as small as possible to get it all in, though there's half a page for each day.

I spy with my little eye something beginning with L.
L for Longleat Man. L for Lunatic.
K for Killer and M for Murderer. B for Balding and
Big Belly.

Then something hits me. What if Longleat Man isn't who I think he is? What if he just *looks* like the man at the police station? And I get this plunging feeling in my stomach, like a great stab of disappointment, because it matters. It matters that I do this thing. If it's not him, then there's no point.

But I can check it out, can't I? I can look him up in the telephone directory. I run down to the hall and I'm crouching on the stairs going through the Ms. Here he is: T. A. Moss, 36 Abigail Road, Norwich. It's him, all right: T. A. Moss and Longleat Man are the same person. Panic over.

I'm just putting it back on the hall table when Mum comes out from the sitting room. She's looking at me hard, like I've got a zit on the end of my nose. Perhaps my eyes are still puffy or something. I turn and start up the stairs because I don't want her to see, but she's put her hand on my arm and she's saying, "Joe? Is there anything the matter?"

I want to tell her, honest. I want to tell her about my plan, but I know I can't because it'll only work if it's secret. And part of me wants to say, yes, Mum— something is the matter because I miss Dad. But I know that nothing's going to bring him back and if I start talking, I'll start blubbing and then she'll blub and it'll make it worse, not better.

So I grunt, "No. Why should there be?"

And she says, "Look, Joe, I'm sorry for shouting at you earlier—you know I don't mean it . . ."

Now she's on the stairs, putting her arm around my shoulder and trying to pull me toward her.

"Come on, Joe. Come and sit with me for a bit—I'll make you a milk shake if you like. . . ."

"Get off!" I shout. "Just leave me alone will you?"

I pull away and run up the stairs because I don't

want to see her face. Can't she see she's only making it worse?

I've finished the diary entry, entered the sightings and all the details. I decide to award myself the maximum twenty-five points.

From now on I'll need to keep the diary in a safe place, away from prying eyes and Tom's sticky little fingers. I find the perfect place. It's my Junior Joker's set, covered in dust from lying under my bed for a zillion years. If I lift out the tray containing all the tricks, the diary slips in underneath. With the tray back in, no one would ever guess. I'd forgotten about this old set. Groveling under my bed is a voyage of discovery. I remember putting the plastic doggy-do on Dad's armchair and practically wetting myself waiting for him to come in and see it. Then in he walks, saying, "Oh no—I can't believe it—what's this on my chair?" Mum comes in too, only you can tell she doesn't think it's so funny: she's having nothing to do with it. And all the time I'm falling about, laughing my head off, thinking he's been taken in. It never occurs to me that, as he gave the set to me for my birthday, he might possibly be fooling. I must have been a right wally. Still, I was only six or something.

I test out the whoopee cushion. It still works. I put the lid back on and slide it under my bed.

I need time to think now: to plan exactly how I'm going to do it, how I'm going to spy on Longleat Man. It was easy today, the first time. But if I make myself too obvious, it won't work. He's going to notice me for sure if I'm just hanging around all the time. Perhaps I can have a collection of disguises. I suddenly get this picture of myself in a black hat, glasses, and a false mustache, wearing a raincoat with the collar turned up, and I can't stop laughing. My headboard is banging against the wall, I'm laughing so much. It's not even very funny, but I just can't stop myself laughing.

I'm going to find out everything there is to know about Longleat Man. He's not getting away with anything. I'll be watching and waiting. I don't think I've ever hated anyone so much. But I only have to think about The Plan and I feel a hundred times better.

Mum's calling that supper's ready. As I make my way downstairs, I remember that today's the last Saturday of the month. It always used to be a special treat on the last Saturday: always a takeaway from McDonald's. Dad would take the orders and him and me would whizz round to the drive-in on the ring road.

Then we'd all sit with trays on our laps in front of the telly watching *Noel's House Party* or *Blind Date*. We don't do it anymore; it wouldn't be the same. That's what really gets me. Every day, when you're least expecting it, it's like there's these glaring great arrows saying PETE HARRIS WAS HERE, reminding you there's a huge chunk missing, leaving a great hole. And sometimes arrows appear for no reason at all, like when I was watching a TV ad for oven chips and the words DAD'S DIED. HE DIED AND HE'S NOT COMING BACK come into my head. Or like the other evening when Richard and Simon are fooling around pretending to be sumo wrestlers and I'm laughing and suddenly I think, I shouldn't be laughing. It's wrong.

It's pizza tonight, but Lucy's playing with hers, pushing it round her plate.

"I thought you liked pizza," says Mum. "I bought it specially."

"I'm just not hungry," says Lucy.

"You've got to eat something, Lucy."

"Why?"

End of conversation.

"Can I have it, then?" says Tom.

Lucy slides it onto his plate. Mum gives one of her extra-long sighs, and Lucy gets up and leaves.

Mum stares out of the window. She's got a nerve, nagging Lucy. She's hardly eaten any of her own.

At the other end of the table, Dad's old place, it's all set out for him: plate, knife, fork, everything. Yeah, you're right; it *is* dead weird.

When Richard came round once, a few weeks after the accident, he sat there by mistake and Tom says, "You can't sit there—it's my daddy's place."

He looked really embarrassed, and it made me feel a total plonker. How do you explain to someone that your four-year-old brother thinks his dead dad is coming back?

I didn't even try. "Just drop it, will you?" I say to Richard later when he asks, "You mean someone forgot to tell Tom?"

It's not that simple. It took me a while to work it out. I had to go right back to see how such a stupid thing had happened: right back to Accident Sunday. Like, there we were, just finishing our apple crumbles, when the doorbell rings. We'd given up waiting for Dad and his wallpaper and started lunch without him.

"Don't tell me he's forgotten his key as well," says Mum, getting up to put his lunch in the microwave. "Tell him he's too late!" she calls out to Lucy, who's gone to answer the door. "The restaurant is closing!"

"It's a policeman, Mum," calls Lucy. Then adds, "I'm off round to Sally's—I'm really late now."

Mum goes out into the hall, Tom jumps down and shoots upstairs, and I help myself to seconds. I'm just finishing when Mum comes back in. She's got her coat half on, half off and she's scrabbling around under the bench for her handbag. Then she's rummaging around on the desk, saying, "Where's my purse?" and trying to hitch her coat on at the same time. Then she looks at me as if she's only just noticed I'm there.

"Listen, Joe," she says. "There's been some sort of accident with Dad's car, so they're taking me to the hospital."

"I'll come with you," I say, jumping up.

"No, Joe." She looks at me and makes an effort to rearrange her face into a sort of smile. "Honestly, love, you'll be a lot more help if you could stay here and look after Tom till I get back. Thanks, love. Now, don't worry—I'll ring from the hospital as soon as I can."

She gives me a peck on the cheek and then she's gone. All the time, the microwave has been giving out its little peep-peeps. Dad's lunch is ready. I go over and switch it off.

Half an hour or so later, Mum hasn't rung yet. I'm

feeling a bit put out, and Dad's food is stone cold. There's another ring at the doorbell, and this time it's Gran and Grandad Watson.

"Oh, you poor love," says Gran, grabbing me toward her so hard that her brooch leaves an imprint on my cheek. I'm getting really worried by now. Perhaps Dad's badly hurt; perhaps they'll have to keep him in. And he's supposed to be helping me make my hot-air balloon for my science project this week. Or perhaps she realizes what I've had to put up with from Tom for the last thirty minutes. I've finally shut him up, though, by letting him play Pinball on my computer.

She asks where Tom is, and I tell her. Grandad's just standing there, studying the picture on the wall, not saying anything. He never says much. It's all he can do to get a word in edgewise sometimes with Gran. Don't get me wrong; she's okay, but she does go on a bit. But then something odd happens. Gran looks at him hard, then rolls her eyes upstairs and tosses her head, like she's got something stuck in her ear and she's trying to shake it out. It's a signal for him to go up and keep Tom out of the way; like I'm not supposed to notice?

Grandad stares at her like she's suddenly lost her marbles, then says, "Oh, right—I'll just pop up and say hello to Tom, then," while Gran takes me by the shoulder and leads me into the kitchen.

I'm getting a bit wound up now. Mum said she'd ring me first, didn't she? I don't need baby-sitting: I can handle it. I can tell now that something is really up, the way Gran is ignoring all the dirty plates and stuff all round the kitchen. Usually she's hardly put her handbag down before she's squirting soap all over the mugs in the washing-up bowl. Mum doesn't take after her at all; Dad was the tidy one.

She starts to twiddle the rings on her finger.

"Your dad had quite a nasty crash, Joe," she's saying. "But they're looking after him—your mum said to tell you not to worry. I mean, doctors these days, it's amazing what they can do—all those machines and things."

I don't like what I'm hearing. But Mum said not to worry. I'm just imagining things. She'd have said, wouldn't she, if he was in any real danger?

"Your mum will ring as soon as there's any news. I'm sure he'll be all right—just you wait and see."

Later, I ask, "Gran, when did Mum ring you, then?"

"Oh, about half past two," she says much too cheerfully.

It's ten to four now and she's been looking at the

clock every few minutes. The kitchen hasn't looked so clean and shiny since she last visited; she even cleaned out the oven. Tom and Grandad have gone up the park and we're sitting here in front of the TV. Don't ask me what it's about. My mind's been on other things.

I hear the police car before I see it, and I'm out of the front door before you can blink.

I know from the moment I see Mum's face. She doesn't have to say a word. And from the way the policewoman with her is looking at us, keeping out of the way. Mum grabs me and she's rocking me, like a baby. But I've got to hear it.

"He's not dead, is he?" my voice is saying. "He's not dead, is he, Mum?"

But she's not saying anything, just shaking her head, her face all screwed up and wet and ugly.

We've hardly gotten indoors when Tom's running in with Granddad behind him and he's shouting, "Hey, guess what, Mum? I beat Grandad three times on Pinball!"

But he doesn't get a chance to say any more, because Gran's got him by the hand and is saying in a voice that sounds like she's being strangled, "Mummy's not feeling very well at the moment, Tommy . . ." She looks over Tom's head at Grandad and shakes her head slowly from side to side. "I bet you the tube of chocolates I've got in my handbag you couldn't beat him again."

"I bet I can," says Tom, running up the stairs without taking his jacket off. Grandad follows him up.

The doctor came after that and gave Mum something, and she went to bed. Gran just took over and they stayed for ages. They were great, really; arranged for Lucy to come home and told her; did everything. But when Tom came running downstairs for his chocolates a bit later, and said, "Where's Daddy? I want to show him how I can do it," she said, "Daddy's had to go away, darling. How about you show me?"

She kept saying it, too. "Don't you worry about it," she'd say each time he asked. "Mummy and Lucy and Joe are all very sad about it too, so we'll all have to try being very brave."

He stopped asking after a while. The funny thing was, at the time I was dead jealous. I'd have given anything then to swap places with him, to believe that Dad had only gone away.

Like I said, Gran just took over. She had to, really. Mum was a mess. Some days we hardly saw her. Another time she poured the tea into the sugar bowl. Lucy started laughing. She was hysterical. Dad dead three days and Lucy laughing her head off: doubled up, she was. Then she just ran out.

Gran arranged the funeral, everything, and sent Tom to stay with Auntie Jill in Yarmouth. "He's too young for all this," she'd say to Mum. "Why worry his head with it all? It's for the best, Carol love."

I'm not sure whether Mum even noticed.

Lucy hates it all. She tried to clear Dad's place away once, started scooping up the knife and fork.

"I can't bear it!" she yells. "It's gruesome. Tell him, Mum!"

But then Tom jumps up and tries to put it back and it's like a tug-of-war, so Lucy just runs out. She's always doing that. It's gotten to the point when you're amazed if she doesn't.

"What harm is it doing?" says Mum later when Tom's in bed. "If it makes him happy? What harm is it doing?"

It's almost as if she wants to believe it herself, like a magic spell: as long as we keep setting Dad's place, it might all be a big mistake.

"Well, Joe, did you, or not?"

"What?"

I look up. Mum's looking at me, waiting for an answer.

"I said, did you remember to post that letter I gave you this morning?"

"Yeah," I lie. I forgot: it's still in my jacket pocket.

Just then, Lucy comes in and starts to make herself a peanut butter and jam sandwich.

"I thought you weren't hungry," snaps Mum.

"I just didn't fancy pizza, that's all," says Lucy.

Sometimes I think I'm the only sane person in this house.

Chapter 3

I've had this brilliant idea. Wait for it: a paper round.

The way I see it, if I'm going to be a spy, I need a cover, don't I? And an alibi. I can't just keep disappearing; Mum's going to get wind of something, plus she's always got me lined up for looking after Tom, or fetching this or that. This way, I've got a good excuse. She might even be pleased when I tell her I'll be earning my own pocket money.

Who takes any notice of a kid delivering papers? The chances are I won't get the round for Abigail Road, but it'll give me a cover. I can just cycle along slowly, after I've done my delivery, with one of those big bags over my shoulder, stopping occasionally to peer inside the bag, as if I'm meant to be there, while all the time I'm observing number thirty-six.

You've got to admit, it's brilliant. It came to me when I heard the Sunday papers flop onto the hall floor.

No one else is up yet. Only Tom, watching *Dapple-down Farm* on TV. I'm dressed, out of the house, and on my bike before he's finished his Rice Krispies. It's not even half past seven yet and it's dead quiet. Most windows still have the curtains closed. There's hardly anyone about: an old man walking a dog and a paper-girl just coming out of number seventy-three. She must be the same one who shoved the paper through our door. I've never even seen her before, which just goes to show what a brilliant idea this is. Delivering the papers, you're almost invisible.

It only takes me twelve minutes and twenty-one seconds to get to Abigail Road, even though it's across town. It's dead quick if you take all the shortcuts, though it'll take longer when there's traffic about.

As I cycle past number thirty-six I see the curtains are still shut; lazy slobs. I almost forget to look at Longleat Man's license plate. I need it for my files. It could do with a clean.

It doesn't take me long to notice that there are no newspapers sticking out of the letter boxes down here. Aha! From this I deduce several possibilities. One, the paperboy or -girl is extremely conscientious and has pushed all the papers through, or two, they haven't been yet; three, no one in Abigail Road takes newspapers; or four, they all get up early around here and they're reading them already. Elementary, my dear Watson.

I reach the end of the road and turn into Percy Road; no sign of a newsagent's anywhere. What to do next? Hang about; there's a tall kid pedaling along toward me with a big, shiny orange bag over his shoulder. I watch him stop and lean his bike against the fence, lift out a paper, and march up the path of number five with it. I make my way back and ask him where the shop is, and he directs me past the King's Head and up the next road off to the right.

It's one of those shops that sells everything: papers, food, milk, toys. It's even got a video section. Vic's Early 'Til Late Store, it's called. I'm just leaning my bike against the window when I hear this thumping noise. My sharply tuned ears tell me it's coming from the great hairy fist that's banging on the inside of the glass and pointing a fat finger at a sign saying DO NOT LEAN BIKES AGAINST THIS WINDOW. I give what I hope is a "sorry" look and prop it against the fence instead.

The owner of the hairy fist is leaning across the counter when I go in, studying the pages of a paper. He's huge. Big is too small a word to describe him. And he's covered in tattoos; you don't just look at him, you read him. I can't take my eyes off a big red heart with MOTHER across his fist when I sense he's looking at me, waiting for me to say something. I haven't made a very good start.

"I was wondering," I say, "if you need another paperboy—like for a morning round—or an evening round—or both—I don't mind—I'm looking, see—I was just wondering if you had a spare round, like."

It comes out in a nervous rattle. It's because I'm nervous.

"I don't believe it," he says, jabbing at the paper with his finger. "Just listen to this—this is my horoscope, right?"

He starts to read it to me.

" 'Any new business transactions that come your way this week are sure to succeed. Go for it. Meanwhile, spoil yourself with something to beautify your home, a painting or a delicate piece of china.' "

Has he gone bonkers?

I say, "Pardon?"

"You're asking for a job, right? That's a business transaction, isn't it?"

"Yes—I suppose." I'm feeling a bit confused.

"What sign are you, then?" he asks.

"Don't know."

"When's your birthday, buster?"

"Er, November fifteenth."

He sucks air in between his teeth as if he's heard bad news.

"A Scorpio, eh? With a sting in the tail. They never let go."

He is bonkers.

He scans down the page.

"Here's yours," he says, and starts to read it out.

" 'A super week for ringing the changes, designing a new look or creating a new image. Go on—make yourself irresistible—and watch out for unexpected gifts.' "

I don't know what to say; not without sounding rude.

Then a woman with curly gray hair who's tidying up the papers calls, "Don't take any notice of him, love."

"Let's have a look, then, shall we?" he says, disappearing beneath the counter and then popping up again with a big thick book. He starts flicking the pages, though in his hands it looks like a pocket diary.

"Funny thing," he says after a moment. "One of our lads is on holiday next week. I was planning to get one of the others to cover. Then what happens? You turn up. Uncanny, isn't it?"

My heart's thumping like mad now because everything seems to be working out just like I planned.

"You'd have to start tomorrow morning, mind. Six forty-five. Sharp."

"Great. Thanks."

Then I remember to ask which streets it covers. He runs his thick finger along the page.

"Up Hannah Street, including the flats in Hannah Court, the top half of Cater Street, and Abigail Road."

My heart gives several extra thumps. I have to stop myself from cheering out loud, but I just nod. "Okay—six forty-five, then."

Just as I turn to go, he calls me back.

"Oi—buster, hold on a jiff. Where you going?"

What have I done? He's not going to change his mind, is he? Don't tell me he's going to change his mind.

"We haven't completed our business transaction, have we? Don't you want to know how much it pays, then? It's the first thing most kids want to know round here, isn't it?"

"Oh, yeah. I forgot," I say, breathing again.

It turns out I get eight pounds a week if I do Sunday as well. Eight pounds!

"You strike a hard bargain, don't you?" he says as he takes my name and telephone number.

Then he asks, "How old are you, then?"

"Thirteen," I tell him. Well, I will be in November.

"Right, Joe," he says, all friendly. "See you tomorrow morning, then."

"Oi!" he calls as I walk away and he tosses me a Snickers. "Unexpected gifts," he says. "The stars never lie, do they?"

As I reach the door another paperboy is coming in, lifting his empty bag off his shoulder.

"Here, Vic," I hear him say. "There was a mix-up with nineteen Cambridge. They got the *News of the World* when they should have had the *Telegraph*. They went on something dreadful—you should have heard them—it's always us who get the blame."

"Never mind," says Tatto Arms. "These things are sent to try us. Don't worry—I'll sort it out, won't I?"

"Thanks, Vic," says the boy.

I walk my bike slowly along Abigail Road, biting my Snickers, taking my time so I can get a long, slow look at thirty-six. The curtains are still closed.

I know for sure now that all this was meant to happen. First, seeing Longleat Man, not just once, but twice, and now the paper round. It's like a pattern, a sort of sign. It's all *meant* to happen, I just know it is. Perhaps Vic's right: it is written in the stars.

Crossing the road, I drop my Snickers wrapper over the hedge into Longleat Man's garden.

Chapter 4

Sunday 28th June

Mum goes ape about paper round, should have asked first, it's too far, what about school etc. etc. etc. Later good old Grandad says a paper round never did him any harm nor Mum either come to that so I can but only if I wear my helmet at all times.

Monday 29th June

Get to 36 by 7:32 A.M.
Deliver *Eastern Daily Press*.
Curtains open but no sign of L.M.
L.M. has been busy Escort clean and shiny (5 points) and snickers wrapper gone (5 points)
Fat gray cat sitting on doorstep. No signs of cruelty but even Hitler was kind to animals.
Name tag says Flopsy (5 points) what sort of

person calls a cat Flopsy? YUK

2 pints milk on doorstep (5 points)

Parking permit on Escort NELSON'S PRINT
WORKS is this where he works? (15 points)
CHECK IT OUT!

Tuesday 30th June

Get to no. 36 by 7:28 A.M.

Deliver *E.D.P.*

Flopsy very friendly feel sorry for it.

Sounds of radio through letter box (5 points)

Wednesday 1st July

Reach 36 by 7:42 A.M. because of a ton of *Radio
Times* with papers

Delivered *E.D.P. Radio Times* and *Women's
Own.*

Door opens and Longleat Woman in dressing
gown bends down for milk, hear her shouting
upstairs Alex are you up yet.

Is Alex the Longleat Kid?

Decide not to give points anymore it's all a bit
pointless, (joke)

Thursday 2nd July

Reach 36 by 7:22 A.M.
Deliver *E.D.P.* and *Autocar.*
Garbage cans out so take quick look in for
evidence. AMAZING. Everything neat in plastic
bags, grab top one and shove in paper bag and
hide in wardrobe till get home from school.

3:43 P.M.
CONTENTS OF RUBBISH BAG
screwed-up envelope used as shopping list KEEP
IN FILE FOR SAMPLE OF HANDWRITING
2 diet yogurt pots
empty tin of Whiskas Liver stuffed with old tea
bags
eggshells
slimy salad
1 1/2 fish fingers
something disgusting wrapped in newspaper.
Remains of mouse?
toilet roll
2 banana skins and 1 apple core
remains of Chinese takeaway
5 Heineken beer cans

wrapping from one pound bar cadbury's whole
nut
bread bag with two crusts
ALL COVERED IN DISGUSTING CIG. ENDS
AND ASH
NO WONDER L.M.'S BELLY IS SO BIG.

Friday 3rd July

Dump rubbish in street bin
Reach 36 by 7:25 A.M.
MAJOR EVIDENCE OF RECKLESS
DRIVING!!!!!! L.M.'s nearside brakelights
SMASHED.
PEOPLE LIKE HIM SHOULD NOT BE
ALLOWED ON THE ROADS!!!!!
Decide to give myself 100 points

Saturday 4th July

Overslept didn't get there till 7:52. Curtains still
closed. BRAKE LIGHTS REPLACED ALREADY!!!
WHY SO QUICK? WHAT'S HE TRYING TO
HIDE?
ALSO!!!! MAJOR DISCOVERY theres a lane runs

along the back gardens—how can I have missed it? Can see through slits in fence at back into garden his stupid garden chairs and one of those barbecue things like a black mushroom on legs.

I HATE HIM!

I pick up my red pen and add ten extra exclamation marks after I HATE HIM. They almost go through the page.

I've read it through I don't know how many times. Yeah, I know it doesn't sound like much. That's because I can't put into words what it feels like when I'm right there, pushing the paper through the door with the black plastic three and six. It's a feeling of—power. There's just this thin bit of wood between me and him. All that separates us is the door or a layer of bricks or a pane of glass. And knowing that *he* doesn't know that I'm there, watching and waiting. I can feel this power growing and swelling inside me, like I could just point a finger at him and he'd explode. BANG!

Sometimes, when I'm standing there, looking at his stupid Escort with his stupid sticker, I try to get into Dad's mind and imagine what it must have been like to see L.M.'s ugly mug grinning at him over the steering wheel. I just hope that wasn't the last thing he saw. No one deserves that.

I'm building up a really strong picture of Longleat Man now. I can just see him, stuck in front of the telly, slurping up his Chinese, guzzling back his beer and stubbing out his cigarettes in the fried rice. I'm almost beginning to feel sorry for the Longleat Kid.

I hope they put him away for life.

I pick up my pen and add to my diary:

I HAVE THE POWER.

Chapter 5

I reckon I could write a book called *Things Every Kid Should Know Before Taking On A Paper Round.*

There'd be a big color photo on the first page showing the permanent scar on the shoulder from lugging around a ton of papers and magazines and a close-up of blackened and scarred hands. My Supply List would include American football shoulder pads, steel-tipped gloves to deal with booby-trapped letter boxes and yappy dogs, a jungle jacket, a forklift truck for loading up the bag, and a crowbar for forcing the papers through all those stupid little letter boxes. I could do a whole chapter on dogs. And fussy customers. And sisters who say when you stagger home like a zombie, D'you mean to say you get £8 a week just for that?

I've just spent light-years standing here, separating all the bits of *The Sunday Times,* the *Observer,* and the *Independent* so that I can feed them through a letter box the size of a postcard at number twelve Cater Street. They can't be normal; this is half a rain forest. This is a major overdose. Just as I'm slipping the last bit in, I get a nasty feeling. This is not the time to realize that these were for number eight. I scrabble in my bag and see that number twelve should have had the *Sport on Sunday*. Never mind. As Mrs. Austin our teacher is always telling us, try to broaden your reading habits. I walk on and slip the *Sunday Sport* through the letter box of number eight. It's my last day anyway.

"You know what you want to put on that?" Vic is saying to Gemma when I get back to the shop. Gemma, one of the papergirls, is unwinding a bloody tissue from her finger.

"Cobwebs," says Vic. He likes to answer his own questions.

"Get away," says Gemma.

"No, straight up," says Vic. "Read it in a magazine. It's what they used in olden days for healing cuts and that. Works a treat, don't it?"

"I don't know why you waste your time, reading all that rubbish," says Shirley. She's the gray-haired lady who works here sometimes.

"I'll stick to Band-Aids, thanks," says Gemma, wrinkling her nose and wrapping her finger up.

"Sounds painful," says Vic.

I follow Gemma into the back of the shop where we hang up our bags. That's it, then.

Vic's waiting for us when we come out, counting out our wages. I reckon I've earned every penny.

"Next time I'll leave his rotten paper on the path— his letter box is lethal," says Gemma, pocketing her money and leaving.

"Fancy her, then?" says Vic, wobbling his eyebrows up and down as she clangs the door.

"Leave it out," I say, and I can feel my face grow warm. Gemma's twice my size.

"No, you're right," he says. "Don't do to mess with older women."

I catch sight of my silly grinning face in the glass of the cigarette shelves.

He's all right, is Vic. Once you get used to him: all these bits of information he finds in the stuff he reads in the shop and the way he talks in questions.

"Right, then," he says, slamming the till shut and handing me a little bag of money. "See you tomorrow, then."

"No—it's my last day. You only took me on for the week," I say.

"Didn't I tell you, then?"

"Tell me what?"

"Hang on."

I have to wait while he deals with a man who didn't get his color supplement.

"He's deserted me," he says as the man leaves.

"Who?"

"Steve—the one who's round you've been trekking—he was made an offer he couldn't refuse, wasn't he? Trolley duty at Sainsbury's."

"Yeah?"

I can't believe my luck. It's not that I get pleasure from dislocating my shoulder every morning, but it's worth it if it means I can keep Longleat Man permanently close up in my sights.

"So, we'll be seeing you tomorrow, then?"

"Yeah, thanks, Vic."

"Fancy me forgetting that. Is my memory going or something?"

He taps his head.

"Oi," he calls as I wait to get past a woman bending over a pile of *Sunday Express*es. "Did you know there was a man who could recall the exact order of six packs of shuffled playing cards? Amazing, eh?"

Shirley rolls her eyes at me. The phone starts to ring, and Vic picks it up.

"What's the address?" he says. "Twelve Cater Street?"

I make a quick exit.

"You're in a good mood," says Mum.

She's got a funny look: pleased but suspicious. All because I've offered to take Tom to the park.

"It's the holidays, isn't it?" I say. "Who wouldn't be now that school's finished?"

"I like school," says Tom.

"How do you know?" I say. "You haven't even started yet. It's not like playgroup, you know. You don't know what you've got coming. One day you'll look back on this as the best time of your life."

"Joe!" says Mum. "Don't take any notice of him, Tom. He's only joking. You'll love it when you start in September. Just you see."

The truth is, I was dreading the summer holidays. All those glaring arrows pointing to the holes Dad's left. It's different now. I've got other things to do and no school getting in the way. There's nothing standing between me and Longleat Man. I've got all the time in the world.

"On the pavement, Tom!" I yell.

"You're riding on the road," he says.

"Yeah, well, I'm not four, am I?"

"Daddy lets me."

It's a good job I'm feeling generous. I suppose I was feeling a bit sorry for him, seeing him sitting on the landing dangling his legs through the banisters, dressed up in his Virgil Tracy Thunderbirds outfit with no one to rescue.

"Where's Matthew, then?" I say as we reach the park gates. "Is he on holiday or something?"

"I don't like him anymore," says Tom, dropping his bike and running off toward the slide.

I catch him off the end a couple of times and swing him round and bounce on the seesaw with him when he sees one of his friends from playgroup and they disappear into the sandpit.

I practice my slow bike ride along the path. The hardest bit is keeping your balance, jerking the pedals just enough to keep you moving without falling off. It's not as easy as it looks. It gets boring after a bit, so I go and yell at Tom that it's time we left, but he doesn't want to go. He's playing Tarzan on the rope ladder, so I stretch out on the grass and take in the scenery. I ought to get good marks in heaven for this.

I've been thinking about that lately: heaven. Whether or not it's just a big con by parents and teachers to make you toe the line. You know, a bit like Fa-

53

ther Christmas; how Mum used to say to Lucy and me from the beginning of December onward, when you wouldn't tidy your room or go to bed, "Well, I just hope Father Christmas isn't watching."

I sort of think there must be. Heaven, not Father Christmas. I can't believe everything just gets snuffed out. Dad wasn't just a body. Where's the rest gone?

What bothers me, if there is a heaven, is what Dad's going to do all day. What he really liked was mending things: clocks, toasters, toys, hair dryers. People were always giving him things to mend. They're still on the shelf in the dining room. Waiting. Nothing's going to need mending in heaven, is it? Not if everything's perfect. And who's he got for company? He'd want us, wouldn't he? He must miss us just like we miss him. I've been racking my brains to think who he might bump into. There's Nan Harris, Dad's mum. But I'm not sure if that's good or bad news. You just couldn't ever please her. When you visited she'd moan all the time that no one ever visited, and when you took her out she'd moan that she was missing *Pot Black* or *Highway* and a decent cup of tea. Dad said loads of times, "That's it—the last time—I'm never taking her out again." He always did, though. Then there was old Mr. Cope next door, but the only time he ever spoke to us was to shout at me not to ride on the pavement and when he cut the branches of our tree and threw them over the fence, calling out, "Yours, I believe." Heaven's not all it's cracked up to be; not when you think about it.

"My mum says you get piles if you lie on damp grass."

I look up. It's Richard.

"Piles of what?"

"I dunno, but she always says it. She says it about leaning against radiators, too."

He throws his bike down and joins me.

"What you doing, then?"

"Nothing much—looking after Tom." I nod in the direction of the playground.

"I called for you yesterday," says Richard. "And on Tuesday."

"I was out."

"I know that. And at the weekend."

He looks at me sideways under his pale eyelashes, waiting for an explanation.

"What would you rather be?" I ask. "Boiled alive in chocolate or tickled to death?"

"Mmmm," he says, flopping back, frowning in concentration. "Tricky."

This is our "What's worse?" game. We've been play-ing it for years. You have to choose and explain why.

"The thing is, being tickled to death could last for days—it'd be agony. And it depends who's doing the tickling and where. I think I'd rather be boiled alive in chocolate. You could eat as much as you liked and end it all quickly by drowning yourself," says Richard.

"I forgot to tell you," I say, "that you're tied to a post with your head above the chocolate line."

"Blast! That's different."

I'm just weighing up the advantages of being a head louse or a slug when Tom rides over and says he's bored and wants to go home.

"How about this afternoon, then?" Richard asks. "We could go swimming."

"No, sorry—can't. I'm busy."

"You're always busy," he says. "What's going on?"

"Would you rather be sucked to death by a giant spider or swallowed slowly by a python?" I say.

Gran's here when we get back. I can hear her in the kitchen helping Mum set the table for lunch. She often pops in on Fridays when Grandad's at his bowling club.

"It's for the best, Carol," she's saying loudly. "There's no need to say anything at all. Don't worry— your dad and me will come with you. Why cause any more—"

But the second she hears me and Tom in the hall she's rattling along different lines. "So I said to the girl, call this a shoe shop? Haven't you got anything navy in a wide fitting?"

My pen's run out, so I'm searching around in the desk drawers in the dining room. I don't really know why it's called the dining room. We never do any dining in here. Except at Christmas. And funerals. Dad used to sit in here and do his bills and things and Lucy uses it for her clarinet practice and sometimes I use the table when my friends come round and we play Blood Bowl or Warhammer, but I haven't done that for ages now. Anyway, these walls have a high embarrassment rating. They're covered in our old school photos, even one of me at a playgroup party dressed as a gnome. On a scale of one to ten, that rates twenty.

I'm just going through the bottom drawer and wondering why Mum keeps all our old birthday cards when my ears prick up. It's Mum and Gran in the kitchen. Gran's been prattling on for ages about someone called Edie and the trouble she has with her legs. I haven't really been listening, but now Mum is saying, ". . . just never in. I don't know where he's going— what he's doing. He tells me he's at Richard's, but I know it's not true—he called round yesterday and said he hadn't seen Joe for ages. And he didn't get home till nearly ten on Wednesday."

"Why ever didn't you tell me, Carol? How long has this been going on?"

There's a long pause and the sound of tea being poured.

"Well, about the time he started that paper round. I'm that worried, Mum."

"He's taken it hard, Carol. It can't be easy, losing a father at that age . . ."

"It's hard for all of us, Mum. And this paper round—what does he need the money for? He doesn't buy anything—not that I know of. There's nothing new in his room—not that I can see, anyway. Where's it all going? There are only a few coins in his money box. And I can't get near him these days."

A cup rattles on its saucer.

"Now, don't get me wrong . . ." It's Gran. "But you read such terrible things in the papers . . ."

"What things, Mum?"

"Well—you know—drugs and suchlike."

"Drugs? Mum! He's twelve!"

"And these whatnots—one-armed bandits—slot machines. There was a whole page about it in the paper. Children as young as ten, mark you—taking money from their mother's purses . . ."

She goes on for ages about it.

Then Mum's voice. "I just don't know what to think—if only he'd talk to me."

"He's not looking himself. I said to Dad the other day, Reg, Joe's not looking himself. Washed out—that's how he looks."

"Perhaps I need to be a bit firmer with him," Mum is saying.

"Well, Pete wouldn't have stood for it—I know that. You always were a bit soft, Carol, if you don't mind me saying."

The chairs scrape back and there's the sound of crockery.

"If you want my advice, Carol—I'd put an end to this paper round nonsense. Make him stay in a bit more and—"

I don't hear the rest. I run through the hall, slamming the front door behind me, grab my bike, and pedal down the road, not even turning to look at Mum, who's running down the path and calling me.

What do they want from me? To be like Lucy, shut up in her room most of the time, feeling sorry for herself, or flopped in front of the TV? Or like Tom, with his stupid magic plate waiting for Dad to materialize? I don't go crawling into Mummy's bed in the middle of the night, do I? And who is it that fixes the video?

Who wired the plug onto the new toaster? And who wheels the garbage cans out every Monday morning? WHO IS IT?

What do they know? NOTHING.

And what does Gran mean with her stupid "Pete wouldn't have stood for it"? He'd be PLEASED. He'd be proud. I'm the only one actually doing anything. And it's for them I'm doing it. Not just for me.

He'd be pleased that I found my way to Nelson's to check that Longleat Man worked there. Pleased that I slip over to thirty-six in the evenings to check whether his Escort's in or out. It's all in the diary. I know what TV he watches even, because I've seen it flickering through the curtains. I've seen the Longleat Kid leave for school and get home, and I know that Longleat Woman works at Kwick Dry Cleaners. I know the color of his disgusting underpants and Alex's naff pajamas because I've seen them flapping on the line. I've even sat in one of his poxy garden chairs when everyone was out. I know . . .

I'm here. I don't remember getting here, but here I am, in the lane by the back gate of thirty-six. They don't lock it. I forget how many times I've slipped in and checked it out. Only when it's safe, mind: when I've watched them all leave. I can see they've got a new fancy umbrella thing over the table in the garden. Wait a minute. There's someone coming out of the back door: the Longleat Kid. He goes into the shed, then comes out again with his bike. But it's not his old Raleigh. He's coming toward the back gate.

I turn my wheel and slowly pedal away. I hear the back gate crash shut and feel a draft of air as he overtakes me on a new ridgeback—it's a Trek 850. That's got to be four hundred pounds' worth, at least. I hope someone steals it.

It's past eight when I get home. The minute I step in I hear Mum call, but I ignore her and run upstairs to my room to dig out the old Ferrero Rocher box where I now keep all my money, away from Tom's nosy fingers. It's in my old gym bag.

I go slowly down the stairs and hand it to Mum, who's standing at the bottom.

"Forty pounds," I say. "Check it if you like. Five weeks at eight pounds a week."

Then, to rub it in, "I was saving up. You're always saying how money's short now. I was going to give it to you just before Christmas."

"Oh, Joe," she's saying, and she's all over me. I

wanted to walk away at first because I thought that she'd set me off too. But I surprised myself. I feel in control. I'm saying, "Don't worry, Mum. Everything's going to be okay."

Chapter 6

I've got an evening round as well now: Chris, who used to do it, chucked it in. It's the same route but delivering the *Evening News*; lightweight and quick, and I get another £5 a week on top. They don't take the *Evening News* at thirty-six, but it gives me a chance to cruise past and take in the situation. Anyhow, it's better than being at home. It's become— what's the word when you feel shut in? Claustro-phobic, that's it. It's the way Mum looks at me: sometimes I can feel her eyes boring through me. She doesn't say much, though. Apart from that night when I came home and gave her my forty pounds. She wouldn't take it, so I shoved it in a jam jar and stuck it on the desk as a reminder that she didn't trust me.

"Just tell me, Joe," she says, "where you go when you're out. I understand if you need to be on your own. I'm sure you wouldn't do anything silly. But I have to know where you are."

"There's this other kid I've got to know," I say. "We have a lot in common."

She looks relieved: the stiff look in her face has gone.

"A friend? Why didn't you say? Do I know him? What's his name?"

"Alex," I say. "I see a lot of him lately—I hang round his place quite a bit."

"Well, why don't you bring him home sometimes? Invite him to tea if you like."

"It's a bit difficult. He doesn't know . . . about Dad. It'd mean questions—you know . . . I just don't like talking about it. I just need to get out."

She's holding me by the shoulders now and nodding. "I do understand, Joe," she's saying. "Whatever you may think. I just wish you'd talk to me occasionally—it might help."

She's watching me hard.

I pull away.

"Where does he live, then, this Alex?"

"Near the shop. I often stop by when I do my round."

She nods. "Okay, Joe, if that's the way you want it.

Just promise me one thing; you are telling me the truth, aren't you?"

"Yes, Mum. Honest."

I was right, wasn't I? Every word was true: not a single lie. And every time Mum looks at me that way she has, as if she's asking something without opening her mouth, I remind myself that every word was true.

I don't have to be at Vic's till four, but I've gotten into the habit of getting there early. A few of us do. Sometimes we help mark up the papers or tidy up or get the latest advice from Vic. He's going on about circles in cornfields at the moment: he reckons it's aliens.

I pedal past the back gate of thirty-six, like I always do on the way in, and stop to peer through the fence. I almost fall off my bike as a great crashing sound against the other side of the fence sends me stepping back. Then there's a shout, and when I look through a few seconds later I can see Longleat Man sitting on his chair, yelling and stabbing a finger toward Alex, who's balancing a ball on his foot, real expert like, and pretending he's not listening, while Longleat Man is ranting on about what the hell does he think he's doing, he didn't plant flowers for him to kick to bits and does he know how much a new fence panel costs. Then, suddenly, without a word, Alex kicks the ball so hard it rebounds off the wall into next door's garden. He grabs his bike that's leaning against the wall and heads toward the back gate. It's time for me to go. I hear the back gate crash, and when I look round he's pedaling like fury in the opposite direction, only this time he's on his scruffy old Raleigh.

They deserve one another, if you ask me. Seeing them look so miserable has really cheered me up.

I go over the details so they're fresh for my diary. L.M.'s been home all week now. His Escort's there every time I look. Haven't seen much evidence of all this gardening he claims to do, though. From what I've seen, it's Longleat Woman who wields the lawn mower and trundles the wheelbarrow. He's a total slob and his belly's bigger than ever.

I peer in again on my way back home. The slob's fallen asleep in his chair.

I can't believe we're nearly four weeks into the summer holiday. Where's it all gone?

It's good here by the river; it gives me space to think and I never see anyone I know; I don't spend all my time at thirty-six. I've got it down to a fine art now, just enough so that I don't get noticed. James Bond could learn a few things from me. I wouldn't mind his transport, though.

A couple of ducks are waddling over to me. They're not stupid: they've noticed me opening up the chicken sandwich I've just bought.

"Quack off!" I say. "Buy your own."

Anyway, I think, there's a moral issue here, feeding chicken to ducks. It'd be like cannibalism. It could lead to all sorts of problems once they'd got the taste.

A cruiser chugs slowly past. You can tell they're holidaymakers: none of them have their life jackets on and they're all wearing little sailor caps with "Captain" printed on them.

"And this . . ." I hear a loud voice behind me ". . . is where the Normans constructed a waterway from the River Wensum to the site of the cathedral—the spire of which you see behind me. The stone for the building being brought by boat all the way from Caen, in France, in 1069 . . ."

It's a large lady towing a group of tourists. I know all of this. We did the Norman Conquest last year. The best bit is when King Harold gets shot in the eye with an arrow. She ought to tell them that bit.

"Can you hear me at the back? Dooo say," the woman is asking. Everyone can hear: even the couple strolling along on the opposite bank who have stopped to listen. She leads the group off along the path toward the cathedral.

It's funny, this, because it reminds me of a totally weird dream I had last night. Dad was in it too. Not the old dream, where I'm walking toward him but, just as I get close, I find myself moving away from him. I look down and I see we're standing on this great slab of ice which is breaking up into pieces. So I jump onto the next bit and get a bit closer, but that breaks up too, and I'm leaping from one to the other and they're getting smaller and smaller and I start to slip into the water, and all the time Dad's watching motionless as I drift away clinging to a tiny chunk of ice. Then I wake up in a cold sweat.

Last night's dream was completely different. Somehow, I'd got to heaven; it was very bright but sort of misty, so you couldn't see your feet. I'm standing there, trying to see Dad among all the people that are strolling past, when along comes Elvis Presley wearing that white suit you see in his old pictures, the one with the big, stand-up collar and flapping trousers and glittery bits. Then I see Dad, jogging in shorts and a vest. But the daft thing is, I'm not interested in him. I'm more interested in Harold. This is *the* Harold, King Harold of Battle of Hastings fame, who has just strolled past. I can tell it's him because he's got a bandage across his eye and he's looking a bit fed up, just like he does in that tapestry thing. Well, he would, wouldn't he? So I run up to Dad, and he doesn't stop or even seem surprised to see me, so I have to run along beside him, and I'm saying, "Hey, Dad, could you get King Harold's autograph for me—it'd look great in my folder and it's worth five credits at least. Go on, Dad."

And without even looking at me, he says, "I'll think about it."

He was always saying that: "I'll think about it." Sometimes he thought so long you'd forgotten what it was in the first place.

Then I woke up feeling really angry with him. I said it was weird.

It's half past three when I get to Vic's today. He's telling a customer who's got a large leafy plant under her arm a story about a woman who bought a pot plant and the next day discovered a dead tarantula in it. It turns out this is a female tarantula and there are all these spider eggs hatched out and by next morning she's finding tarantulas in her bed, her bath, her cornflakes, her slippers, everywhere. Me and Gemma have stopped to listen, giving the woman with the plant a wide berth.

Shirley and Maureen, the other assistants, are meanwhile dealing with the queue of customers, but no one's rushing—they're all ears.

"True," Vic's saying, "as I'm standing here. Read it in a paper so it's got to be, hasn't it?"

"What sort of plant was it?" asks the woman, who has now put her plant on the counter, at a safe distance.

We wander out to the back. The piles of papers are already marked up, so we only have to take our own. You have to slide them in the bag so the street and number are at the top. Just as I'm slipping them in I see a small photo at the bottom of the page which makes me freeze. I'd recognize that face anywhere. It's Longleat Man. And underneath it says "Nightmare Over."

"You coming, then?" says Gemma. Stu and Martina have arrived now, and it's getting crowded in here. I read the next line: *Today, at Norwich Crown Court, Mr. Terence Moss was cleared of causing Death by Reckless Driving.*

I feel sick. The words move around in front of my eyes: they don't make sense. I can't read the rest.

"Joe? You all right?" It's Gemma.

"No. I feel sort of sick—I've got to go. Tell Vic for me, will you?"

She runs out, and I grab the top paper off the pile, stuff it down my sweatshirt, and follow her, pushing past her and the queue of customers. I can't breathe; I need air. I grab my bike and go.

I find my way to the river and throw myself onto the grass behind some bushes. It's a while before I can make myself take out the paper. I've been telling myself all the way here that I've read it wrongly. If I don't read it, then it hasn't happened. I'm as stupid as Tom with Dad's plate.

Even now that I've got it spread out on the grass in front of me, I can't look at the words: I'm putting it off as long as possible. I stare at his ugly face and let the anger and hate build up inside me. It helps somehow. How has this happened? How can he have gotten away with it? He's a murderer. He's the man who killed Dad, and the ugly fat slob's gotten away with it. He's smiling, he's actually smiling, like it's funny. It's not right! It's not fair! He should have got life. Why has it been allowed to happen? What about the police and the court? All this waiting and then they let him go. How can it happen?

I'm lying here, facedown, dribbling and grizzling into the grass. I go over and over it. What gets me, what really gets me, is why wasn't I told? Why do I have to read it in the paper? What if I hadn't seen it? I might never have known.

I sit up, wipe my face on my sleeve, and start to read, slowly:

Today, at Norwich Crown Court, Mr. Terence Moss was cleared of causing Death by Reckless Driving. The accident, which occurred last February in Manor Road, involved another car driven by Mr. Peter Harris of Norwich. Mr. Harris sustained serious injuries from a collision with a telegraph pole. He died shortly after his arrival at the Norfolk and Norwich Hospital. On leaving the court with his wife, Mr. Moss said, "I'm just relieved this nightmare is over."

Is that it, then?

I shove the paper down my sweatshirt and grab my bike. I don't even look where I'm going, shooting out onto the road between a bus and a van. The driver hoots his horn and flashes his lights, but I don't care.

By the time I reach the end of our street my shirt's sticking to me. Granddad's car is parked outside. Well, it would be, wouldn't it? They're all in it together. Those words of Gran's all make sense now: "Why say anything, Carol? Dad and me will come with you."

They knew; they've known all this time.

I throw my bike onto the drive and go in. They're in the kitchen, round the table. I should have known something was up this morning when Mum was wearing her best dress and earrings and makeup. How can I have been so thick?

I pull out the *Evening News* and throw it down on the table, sending Gran's teacup tipping and slurping, running onto the table and dripping into her lap.

"What the—?" cries Gran. But Mum knows what. She's looking at me and at the paper. She knows. Gran's up and fetching the dishcloth from the sink.

"Why?" I'm yelling. "Why? How come you didn't tell ME? He was MY father! I should have been there— I'm not a kid!"

"How dare you speak to your mother like that?" Gran's saying, dabbing at the table. "Can't you see the state she's in? It's bad enough that—that creature— gets off scot-free without you—"

"Shut up! Shut up!" I'm yelling. "You stupid old woman! You and your 'it's for the best.' What do you know about it?"

That shuts her up. She looks at Mum, but she's just sitting there with her head in her hands. Grandad's getting up slowly and saying, "Come on, Ellen—I think we've done enough."

"What?" Gran's openmouthed.

But Grandad's picking up her handbag and pushing her out into the hall. Then, in a voice that I've never heard before, like he's giving an order, he says to me, "See to your mother, Joe."

It's just the two of us, sitting at the table. You can hear the silence. The tea in the cups has gone cold. I start to pick at the coils of the table mat.

"Where's Tom?" I ask.

"At Matthew's." Mum takes a tissue from her sleeve and wipes her face.

"What? They're friends again?"

She nods. She looks terrible: big black smudges under her eyes.

"You look terrible," she says to me.

"What about Lucy?"

"She's working today—you know, at the coffee shop."

"She didn't go to the court, then?"

"No—she didn't want to."

"You told her, then. Why didn't you tell me? I wanted to go! It's important to me." My voice sounds like a croak.

She starts to say something, shrugs, and stops, tugging the tissue between her fingers.

"You seem so—well, so contained. I know that you

don't like talking about it. Don't get me wrong—I understand. I thought that's how you wanted it—not to keep being reminded. It's your way of dealing with it. I felt, we felt, it would only make things worse for you."

"It's for the best, Carol love," I mimic.

She gives a little laugh, then starts to cry again.

"You'll have to apologize, Joe. She'll be very upset."

"I know . . . I hate him," I say. "I really hate him."

"So do I, Joe," she says. "So do I."

Chapter 7

I'm just relieved this nightmare is over. That's what he said, Longleat Man. Well, lucky for some. Some stupid court decides he's not guilty and everything's okay. Back to normal; for him, that is. What about us? It's not over for us, is it? Does he know what it's like when you open your eyes in the morning thinking, perhaps it was all a nightmare and in a minute you'll wake up? But you don't.

I can't sleep. It's nearly 1:20, but I can't sleep; I'm too angry. I don't want to anyway. I'd rather use my time like now, imagining what I'd do if I could get my hands on him. The best is when I've tied him up so he can't move and I'm driving a tank toward him; he's watching helplessly as I edge toward him, till I can see the fear in his eyes and he's begging and pleading with me to stop. So I make him say sorry for what he's done, to me and Mum and everyone, over and over again, on his knees, then just as he's looking relieved I let the tank roll slowly forward.

My thoughts are interrupted by the sound of a door opening, so I leave him there in suspended animation with the tank pressing up against his nose while I listen to the footsteps padding down the stairs. It's Mum: she can't sleep either.

I pick up my diary and read it through again. If I'd known the court case was coming up, I could have given evidence, couldn't I? About that smashed brake light. It's proof he's not safe, isn't it? I could have given them dates and times; it's all down here. But now it's too late. And I start to feel angry again, this time with Mum for not trusting me enough to tell me, when I'm the only one who's actually *doing* anything. How can they sit back and let it happen? They're all so useless. The stupid law has let him get away with murder. There's got to be something someone can do.

I get to the shop a bit earlier than usual to make up to Vic for running out yesterday.

"Don't worry about it," he says. "We managed, didn't we? Just don't make a habit of it, eh? 'Ere, you sure you should be back? You seen yourself in a mirror? It's not catching, is it?"

"No, I'm all right," I say. I'm not in the mood for talking.

I have to make myself walk up the path of thirty-six. It's like it's contaminated. It's like I can see him, his fat, slimy body still slumped in his bed, congratulating himself on getting away with it, a sickly smug smile on his face. He's won and here I am, his slave, delivering his stupid paper. I'm going to chuck the round in. I'll tell Vic today. What's the point anymore? It's all I can do to shove the paper through the door. If it weren't for Vic, I'd tear it up and feed it through in little pieces. I feel like breaking his windows and kicking his door in.

I turn down the path, and as I see his shiny Escort there on the drive, I can feel my front-door key in my pocket. My fingers close round it. I take it out and look at it. Then, slowly, carefully, taking my time, enjoying every inch, I gouge a beautiful thin wavy line in the perfect paintwork, across the hood, along the side, ending with a nice zigzag on the trunk. The curtains are closed. I'm hidden from the road by the hedge. No one can see me. I slip the key into my pocket and take my time to walk down the path, even stopping to get out the *Daily Mail* for number thirty-eight next door. I carefully shut the gate, just like its little metal label asks me to. I feel amazing. I feel calm. I can't stop smiling. I jump on my bike and start to whistle the tune from *Match of the Day*. I won't chuck the paper round; not yet.

For a change, I can't wait to get home. There are so many ideas whizzing around inside my head that I want to get them all down on paper before I forget them.

I plunge under my bed and drag out my diary from the Joker's set. There are blank pages at the back labeled NOTES. I cross it out and write in "The Nightmare Plan." By the time I've finished there's a whole page of ideas; I can hardly write fast enough. And this is only for starters.

I plump up my pillows and lie back to think about it, and the more I think, the more I imagine his face when he sees what's going to happen to him, the more excited I get. More ideas flood into my head, and I have to grab my diary and start another page.

The beauty of it is, it's not like spying when I've got to be there, in person. The Nightmare Plan opens up other possibilities: the phone, sending stuff through the mail; it's brilliant. Why didn't I think of it before? Nothing dangerous, nothing criminal; just enough to get him worried, to make him uncomfortable, so he knows there's someone out there, watching.

Till every day he's wondering what's going to happen next. Every day is a reminder that there's someone who hasn't forgotten what he's done. His nightmare isn't over: it's only just beginning.

I've been busy, really busy. Mum's starting to ask what I've been doing in my room all week. And she's still angling for me to invite "Alex" round. That would be interesting.

I started gently first, just to get L.M. asking, What's going on here? First I went through the piles of magazines and *Radio Times* and color supplements stacked in the garage and cut out all those little coupons. You know, the ones that say "Yes, I am interested in your 7-day plan to make my body beautiful." Or "Please send me my first 'pay-later' volume of *The Complete Works of Shakespeare.*" I've filled in hundreds; I never realized there were so many, asking for agents to call and demonstrate storm windows, fitted kitchens, stone paths, swimming pools, hearing aids; you name it, they're coming. Even a dating agency called Heart-mate. I ticked "Athletic" and "Fashion-conscious" on the coupon.

On Tuesday I borrowed Lucy's Polaroid and took a picture of him getting into his car parked at Nelson's and a blurry one of Longleat Woman taken through the window of Kwick Dry Cleaners. I'm really proud of that one. I wrote "Guilty" on one and "I Am Watching" on the back and sent them by post. I'd just love to see his face when he opens that.

It was the milk on Wednesday; nothing special, just got there a bit earlier, took off the caps, dropped a nice fat worm in one and a dead fly in another, and sprinkled some soil on the top.

Thursday's meant getting up earlier than usual. I reckon he must have started to get a bit wary by now and might be on the lookout in the mornings, so I pedal over there really early, about five-thirty; hardly anyone about. It was so easy: just slipped in and wrote with a thick magic marker over the hood "THIS CAR KILLS." No one even noticed I'd gone. Like I said, I just merge into the background.

Then I got busy with the advertisement for Friday's *Evening News:*

GARAGE SALE,
Sun. 23 Aug. 10:30. at 36 Abigail Road.
Garden Furniture, Barbecue,
Ridgeback Trek 850 Mountain Bike
ALL AS NEW.

Also TV Video and House Contents.
Must Sell, Emigrating.
Nothing More than £30.

But today's, Saturday's, has taken planning. He'll know now; he'll definitely be on the lookout. I can't take chances or risk being seen. This one's going to be a middle-of-the-night job, so I've been lying here in bed, under the duvet since midnight, waiting. For one horrible moment I think I'll have to call it off when I hear Mum go downstairs, but then I hear her come upstairs again. I throw the covers off and tiptoe to the door. Inch by inch, I pull it open and look out onto the landing. The strip of light that was showing under her door has gone. It's time to go. I pick up my trainers and slow-step my way down the stairs. It feels like every nerve is stretched. I can hear every sound; the creak of the banister sounds like a cap going off. There's a moment of panic when I allow myself to think what would happen if Mum came out now and saw me. Would she recognize me? And if she did, how would I explain? There's no way I could convince her I was just getting a drink of water. Not when I'm wearing Lucy's long black skirt and her baggy jumper that I've fished out of the laundry basket. Or her floppy velvet hat I've pinched from the hall stand.

At last I reach the bottom of the stairs. As I let out the long breath I hadn't realized I was holding, I catch sight of a stranger in the hall mirror. It's me, lit by the streetlights shining through the glass of the front door. I tug my trainers on. It's a pity about the trainers: they spoil the effect. I slip out of the front door, using my key to slide the catch, and, taking Lucy's bike from the side of the garage where I placed it ready, I glide silently down the street.

The air feels different: fresh and sharp. No traffic churning out its fumes apart from the rare passing car. I see a few things you don't see in the daytime: the people who sleep in doorways, for instance. One even had a Tesco's trolley piled high with all his carrier bags. Apart from that, it feels like I've got the city to myself; that all the other kids tucked up in bed asleep are missing out on something: the silence, the peace of the empty streets; that it's all mine. I feel I could stay out all night.

It's 1:23 and I'm here by the back gate of thirty-six. I lean the bike against the fence and slip through the gate and head for the front door. The whole thing takes less than a minute. Just a blob of superglue on the bell push and press it in. I hear it ringing as I run round the side and back through the gate and on to the bike and away. As I look back over my shoulder, I see the lights in the upstairs windows glaring in the night and then the downstairs lights come on. By a quarter to two, Lucy's clothes are back in the laundry basket, her hat on the peg, and I'm in my bed. I can still smell the night air on my skin. I feel excellent.

I wake early, like you do when you're excited and looking forward to something, you know, like at Christmas. But I make myself wait and get up at the usual time so that it sounds to anyone who might hear that I'm doing the usual thing. Everything has to appear the same. I don't go past thirty-six on the way in today; I want to save it up, but the waiting's agony. By the time I've finished Hannah Street and Cater as usual, I reach thirty-six at about 7:20. It's like a present I've been waiting to unwrap. It's all I can do to keep a straight face when I see the wires hanging from where the bell used to be. How long did it take them, I wonder, to stop it ringing?

I take my time, searching in my bag for his paper, savoring it all: the scratch mark still on his Escort, the "THIS CAR KILLS" scrawled across the hood. You can see where he's tried to get it off, but it's still there all right. I used a permanent marker.

I'm just aiming the paper toward the letter box

when suddenly the door swings open and there's Longleat Woman shouting, "He's here, Terry! Quick!" and then he's standing there in the doorway, glaring at me. My head's sending out different messages and I don't know which to choose. Has he sussed me out? Should I run? Or should I bawl him out and tell him what I think of him? But how can he know? I've been so careful. Have I overlooked something? Anyway, he can't prove anything.

"Do you do this every morning?" he says.

"What?"

"The paper delivery—are you the boy who does it every morning?" He's starting to shout as if I'm deaf.

"Yeah." I start to relax slightly.

"D'you know anything about this, then?"

He's striding over to the car and banging his hand against the scratch and the lettering, then pointing to the bell push, as if it's all my fault. But by now I know that I'm the only one who knows that.

"Look! Look!" he's shouting. "Someone did this and I want to know who!"

He's working himself up and pushing back what's left of his hair and looking around as if the culprit is hiding under the hedge or something. Then suddenly, Longleat Woman is there again and yelling, "For God's sake, Terry. It's not his fault." Then she turns to me and says, "Look, love, you haven't by any chance seen anyone hanging round here? Someone's been playing nasty tricks. Anyone looking a bit suspicious, around the front door or the car?"

"There was someone," I say slowly. "But I only saw him a few times and not up close. He was in the doorway."

They're interested now, looking at one another and then back to me.

"Can you remember what he looked like?" asks Longleat Woman.

I give them a description. It's a good one. It's the tramp I saw in the Co-op doorway the other night. I smarten him up a bit and I don't say exactly in which doorway I saw him.

The woman thanks me and goes marching back into the house.

"That's it, then!" she's shouting to L.M., who's following her. "If you won't, I will!" and I can see her pick up the phone from the wall.

"You do and I'll—!" shouts L.M. But I don't hear the rest as he slams the door behind him. Then something catches my eye: something through the big front window. It's Alex, the Longleat Kid, and he's throwing a couple of balls into the air as if he can't hear the voices still shouting in the hall. As if none of this is happening.

As I leave, I hold the gate open for the postman, who's struggling through with a great pile of bulging brown envelopes. If I'm not mistaken, everything L.M. needs to know about electric showers, Jacuzzis, burglar alarms, landscape gardening, et cetera, et cetera, and somewhere in there should be an entry form for the Father of the Year Competition.

"There was a phone call for you!" calls Mum when I get back late on Sunday morning. "From Richard— but I think I must have misheard. It sounded like he said he'd rather be swallowed by a python. Does that make any sense?"

"Yeah," I say.

"He said to ring him back," calls Mum up the stairs as I run up to my room.

But I've got more important things to think about. I throw myself onto my bed, laughing, thinking about the jam of cars that I've just seen blocking Abigail Road and the queues of people on the pavement outside number thirty-six, and more cars arriving, while L.M.'s shouting at everyone to get out of his front garden and leave them alone and all the puzzled and angry people wave their *Evening News* at him.

"How many times do I have to say it?" he's yelling. "There is *no* garage sale!"

I get out my diary and decide what to do next. I haven't even warmed up yet.

Chapter 8

It's important not to let up, not for a single day, even if it's just little things with a Big One now and again. He's got to be reminded every day what he's done.

I took most of yesterday, Monday, making the WANTED FOR MURDER poster with the photo I cut out of the *Evening News*. He should have got that by now. And the label off the laundry detergent packet that says REMOVES ALL STAINS—EVEN BLOOD, with blood underlined in red ink.

Friday should be *really* interesting with all those people phoning him when they've seen the For Sale ad I've sent to the *Evening News* for his Escort. It's a bargain: I'm only asking £500.

Today, though, I've been short of time. I've been trailing around the shops with Mum to get all my stuff for my new school. New blazer, shoes, trousers, geometry set, pen, gym kit. And don't forget the haircut; it's impossible to forget the haircut. It's as if she wants to send me off looking as naff as possible. Anyway, I've finished at last, and I left her going to meet up with Gran for a cup of coffee.

I head straight for Vic's to do my evening round, trying to keep my spirits up with what's next on the agenda of the Nightmare Plan. It reminds me that the holiday's nearly over: school starts on Thursday and I'm not going to have so much time. Colman High's not far from here; in fact, I almost have to go past Vic's to get there. Now I come to think of it, it's all worked out neatly. It's another sign.

On my way home I post a box of chocolates to Longleat Man with a label saying "I'm Still Watching." There's nothing wrong with them: they're perfectly safe. But he won't know that, will he?

Mum's still out when I get back, so I head up to my room to bring my diary up to date. Not that there's much to report: they've been keeping a low profile lately. The drizzling weather must have kept them indoors. Though I noticed at the weekend that he's done a cover-up job on his car with a can of spray paint. This is the only time in my life I wish I was a fly. I could hang there on the ceiling watching his face every time the postman brings him a delivery from yours truly, and I could listen to what he has to say on Friday when the phone starts ringing from eager people waiting to buy his bargain Escort.

I see them as soon as I open my door, sticking out from my bed: the empty box, the whoopee cushion, the black soap with its wrapper off next to the rubber chocolate cookie. I leap across and lift out the tray expecting the worst, then flop down, breathing a sigh of relief. The diary's still here. But the relief changes into anger. I know who's been poking around: there's only one person who can't keep his hands to himself.

"Tom!" I yell. "I want you! Now!"

I cross the landing to his room, but he's not there. Or he's hiding. Then Lucy's door opens.

"Do you have to make so much noise?" she says.

"Have you seen what he's done to this?" I yell, waving the box under her nose.

"Is that all?" she says. "I thought it was something serious."

Then, through her door I see Tom sitting on the floor, playing with *my* Guess Who? game.

"Is he wearing a hat?" he says to Lucy, totally ignoring me and staring at all the little heads propped up on the tray in front of him.

"Yes," says Lucy, and Tom flips down all the heads without hats.

"Has yours got glasses?" says Lucy.

"No," says Tom.

"Right," I say, grabbing Tom by the arm and pulling him up. "You go into my room once more and I'll . . . I'll take back all the stuff I've ever given you. And you can forget about ever playing on my computer again! Got it?"

He glares at me.

"And what have you done with my dog's mess? You'd better find it, or else. Now!" I yell, tapping the dog's-mess-shaped space in the plastic tray where it should be.

He looks round at Lucy, then slowly walks over to her bed, gives me another black look, and pulls back the covers. There, sitting in the middle of the sheet, is *my* dog's mess.

He stands there with his hands on his hips.

"You spoil everything, you do!" he shouts.

But Lucy is rolling around on the floor, laughing her head off.

"You should see your face," she's gasping. "It's so serious."

And she rolls from side to side, pulling her knees up.

"Yeah, well . . ."

I can see myself in Lucy's long mirror, and I do look kind of stupid.

"He still shouldn't go poking round in my room. It's private. You'd better learn that, Tom. I'm fed up with it. You wait till Mum gets home."

But I know she won't do anything. She never does.

"I know one thing," I add, because now I'm feeling angry with Mum for being so soft, "Dad wouldn't have let you get away with it."

Lucy sits up and gives me a warning look.

Tom goes back to his Guess Who? game, his back to me.

"You can't tell him," he says, "because he's dead."

Lucy and me stare at each other. She pushes back the hair from her face and hooks it behind her ears and leans toward Tom.

"What did you say, Tom?" she asks.

Tom's staring at all the rows of little heads. I go and sit on the bed so I can see his face.

He looks at me and says, "Daddy was killed. He was in a car crash. Don't you know?"

Then he turns to Lucy and says, "Does he have a mustache?"

"Wait a minute, Tom," I say, joining Lucy on the carpet. "How do you know this?"

"Matthew said," says Tom, looking straight at me. "Does he have a mustache, Luce?"

"Er, yes—I mean no," says Lucy.

And Tom flips down all the heads with mustaches.

"What? Matthew told you Dad was killed in a car crash?" Lucy asks.

Tom nods.

"When?" I say. "When did he tell you, Tom?"

He frowns, then shrugs.

Then something clicks inside my head.

"Was this before the holidays, Tom? Was it that time when you didn't like him anymore?"

Lucy's looking puzzled.

"It might of been," he says. "It's your go, Luce."

"Er, has he got black hair?" she says.

"Nope!"

Lucy knocks down all the heads with black hair, looking sideways at me.

"Is that why you weren't friends anymore, Tom? Is that why?"

Tom's concentrating on the heads again. He gives a slight nod.

"Has he got blue eyes?"

"Er, yes," says Lucy.

There's a click, click, click as he knocks the heads down.

94

"He hasn't just gone away," he tells Lucy as if she doesn't know. "He won't be coming back, ever. You can't when you're killed."

"Why didn't you say before?" says Lucy. "Why didn't you tell Mum you knew?"

"It was too sad," he says. "It makes her cry when I talk about Daddy. She cries in bed sometimes. When she thinks I'm asleep."

We sit here, Lucy and me looking at each other, and I'm looking at Tom like I haven't seen him properly before. My kid brother, who's only four and three-quarters, has been carrying this around all on his own.

Lucy gets up and crouches behind Tom in a sort of hug.

"Listen, Tom, it's true that Daddy was killed. It's just—well, it's just that Mum thought it wouldn't be so sad for you if you thought he'd just gone away."

Tom nods, then looks up.

"Is he in the garden, then?"

"Who?" says Lucy.

"Daddy."

"Daddy? In the garden?"

Lucy looks to me for help.

"You know," says Tom. "Like Oscar and Henry."

We can't help it. Both Lucy and me burst out laughing. I'm thinking. This is wrong: I shouldn't be laughing, but I can't stop, while Tom just stares at the pair of us. Oscar was our cat and Henry was Lucy's old hamster.

"No," says Lucy at last. "You can't bury people in back gardens, Tom. There's a special place called a cemetery." She pauses and looks at me. "We'll take you there one day, if you like."

"Tom," I say. "If you broke friends with Matthew, why did you believe him?"

"I heard Mummy talking to someone on the phone later," he says. "So then I knew it was true. Will they all be together now?" he asks.

"Who?" says Lucy.

"Daddy and Oscar and Henry. You know—in heaven."

I'm just about to tell Tom that there are different points of view about heaven, that there's no actual proof, that I'm not sure myself, but Lucy says, "Yes, Tom. Of course."

Tom nods thoughtfully and looks down at his tray.

"Has he got a beard?" he asks.

It strikes me that the idea of Oscar and Henry ending up in heaven together is kind of interesting. Oscar used to take a very catlike interest in Henry's cage, always sniffing at it and arching his back and trying to get his paw in. It might be heaven for Oscar to have a hamster to chase around forever and ever, but it wouldn't be much fun for Henry, would it? But if he's already dead and just a ghost, then he can't come to much harm, can he? It's getting complicated. It always does when I start to think about heaven.

I pick up the plastic dog's mess from the bed and go back to my room. I take my diary out of the box and slip it under my mattress till I find a safer place for it. Then I put back the soap and the cookie and everything and put the lid on and go back to Lucy's room.

"Here you are," I say to Tom. "I'm too old for it anyway. But look after it. It's special. Dad gave it to me for my birthday."

"Cor, thanks, Joe," he says.

When Mum comes home, Lucy tells her. "He said he didn't want to make you cry, Mum," she explains. So what does Mum do?

Longleat Man has got a lot to answer for.

Chapter 9

I have to get up even earlier this morning, about six, so that I can do my round and get back home in time to grab some breakfast before setting off for school.

I have a weird feeling as I'm walking up the path of thirty-six. It's not just because all the curtains are open, which is unusual, but I know something's missing and I can't quite make it out. Then it comes to me: there's no Flopsy waiting on the doorstep, getting up and arching her back, coming over to rub herself against my legs. And now I come to think of it, she wasn't here yesterday either. I'm searching for number thirty-six's *Eastern Daily Press*, but it's not in the bag. The next one is the *Mail* for thirty-eight, next door. I stand there, straining my ears to pick up any sound from inside, but there's nothing. I know there's no one in; I can sense it; it's got an empty feeling. I duck down and peer through the letter box. I can just make out a bit of

yesterday's *E.D.P.* poking out from under a heap of letters and stuff. No one was here yesterday, then. They
must have gone on holiday—the one to Portugal that
Longleat Woman fancied so much, I bet. And I think
of Mum, whose big treat this summer was a day trip to
London with her friend Lynne, while Gran and
Grandad came over. It's not fair. Then there's all that
work I put into getting the For Sale ad in the paper for
his Escort; all for nothing. The phone will be ringing
and ringing and he won't know a thing about it. He
won't even be here. Well, just wait till he gets back.

I'm exhausted by the time I get home, but I don't
let it show; Mum will start nagging again about giving
it up and school being more important.

My new uniform's all laid out ready. It's so crisp
and new, I reckon it could stand up on its own. By the
time I've got it on I feel like the Iron Man. I can hardly
bend my feet in these shoes, and I'd like to know who
invented ties. What do they actually do, anyway? I
clomp downstairs and inspect myself in the hall mirror.

"Oh, very smart," says Mum. "Don't you think so,
Lucy?"

"Has he forgotten to take out the coat hanger?"
says Lucy, squeezing the shoulders of my blazer.

She's right. It's enormous; it comes down to my knees.

"I bought it on the large side," says Mum. "I want it to last."

But I can tell even she is having doubts, the way she keeps tugging it this way and that. There's a huge gap between my neck and my shirt collar, too, and the blazer sleeves are lumpy where she's turned them up. It's a slight improvement, I suppose. You couldn't see my hands when I first tried it on.

Mum steps back and squints at me as if it doesn't look so bad with restricted vision.

"He'll grow into it," she says, giving the blazer a final tug.

"Not unless he turns into Arnold Schwarzenegger," says Lucy and, grabbing her bag, shoots off.

"Aren't you going together, then?" calls Mum. "I thought that now you're at the same school . . ."

"Now, are you sure you've got everything?" says Mum for the third time. I better have, I think, as I stagger to my bike with my rucksack. I can't get any more in. There's my football kit and boots, tracksuit, gym kit, trainers, cook's apron, art overall, art folder, drawing pad, maths set, pencil box . . .

"Best take it all," Mum says. "You don't want to

find you haven't taken something you need, not on your first day."

By the time I reach Colman High you can hardly see the pavement for blue blazers. Some of these kids are giants; they make me feel like a third-grader. I'm not sure where to go, so I turn my bike toward the gate that everyone seems to be making for and follow a big kid wearing a Walkman who's cycling just in front. All the bikes seem to be heading to the right of the main building. Then I see the rows of bike sheds where other kids are busy chaining up their bikes.

"Oi, watch it, shrimp," says another who walks right into my path.

Just as I'm padlocking it up, Richard and Simon and Jonathan turn up. Richard doesn't say anything at first, just gives me a slow look. Jonathan grabs me by the collar of my blazer, peers down, and calls, "Hello! Is there anyone in there?" and they all laugh.

"My shoulders don't half ache," complains Richard. "Do we really need all this stuff?"

"My mum said I had to bring it all, just in case," says Simon.

"Try and look as if we know where we're going," he says as we follow the crowd toward the playground area. "They might think we're second years."

"Oh, yeah?" says Richard. "With these knife creases in our trousers? Anyway, it's not second year anymore, it's year nine, and we're year eight."

Beyond the playground stretch the school fields and on all sides are more buildings. Everyone is heading in different directions.

"It's huge," says Simon. "I'm going to get lost. I know I'm going to get lost."

We decide to hover around here somewhere and hope that someone tells us where to go soon.

Jonathan pulls a packet of Rolos from his pocket, neatly removes one, pops it into his mouth, and takes his time in folding back the paper and putting it back into his pocket. "Mmmm," he says, watching us watch him.

"Share them out, then," says Simon. "That's what friends are for."

"You've got to be joking."

But quick as a flash Richard grabs them out of his pocket and runs off with them. Running backward, he makes a great show of helping himself to one and then tosses them to Simon.

"Here, Simon. Have a Rolo," he shouts.

"Oi, give them back!" yells Jonathan, running after them, but they dodge him, while Jonathan, weighed down by his giant rucksack, jumps helplessly up and down as they toss them back and forth like a game of piggy-in-the-middle. "Quick!" says Simon, running over to me and holding out the Rolos.

But I can't be bothered. It's a silly kid's game. When are they going to grow up?

"No, thanks," I say. I pick up my bag and start walking toward the bathrooms. I don't feel part of them anymore.

A bell goes. All the new kids are led into the main hall. The Headmaster introduces the Head of Year Eight and then she introduces the year-eight teachers. She's been waffling on about high standards and how rules are for our benefit and how smart we all look and the unsuitability of trainers for school and how we're all going to love it here . . .

The boy sitting next to me is reading *The Citadel of Chaos* hidden behind his binder; I did that one ages ago. I wonder if he's met the Sewer Snake yet? That's another one for Longleat Man, the Sewer Snake. It'll make a change from being squashed by a tank. It will be my slave and do anything I command it: anything I desire. I can send it wriggling up the drains to Longleat Man's bath; just as he's reaching for the soap, its terrible head will rear out of the water and . . .

Suddenly everyone starts to shuffle about and to

murmur, and the teachers are standing up and coming forward.

"What's up?" I ask the boy with the book.

"Don't ask me," he says, shrugging.

There's a girl on the other side, so I ask her. She tells me that the teachers are going to call out the names for their tutor groups and we have to get up and follow them out of the hall to our classes.

I sit, watching them slowly disappear. Jonathan goes off with a teacher in a tracksuit. Lucky kid; he's got the PE teacher. At last I hear my name called: "Joseph Harris, Paula Jenks, Julie Livingstone, Alex Moss, Kim Mumford, Richard Prescott . . ."

Alex Moss? I turn round. I know that thick straw-like hair and that walk, head down and hands stuck into his pockets. I was wrong about one thing, though: they can't have gone on holiday. And I was wrong about something else too: he can't be that much older than me. I'm going to be in the same class as the Longleat Kid.

Chapter 10

It's a relief, really, I think as we follow the teacher along a hundred miles of corridor. It means that Longleat Man is still around. So where are they, then, if they're not at thirty-six? The teacher leads us out of a door and across an open space to what she calls a mobile classroom. It doesn't look very mobile to me. It looks as though nothing but a bomb would shift it.

We pile in and grab somewhere to sit. Jonathan and Simon have disappeared in other directions, so I sit next to Richard, who's in the same class as me. I've lost sight of the Longleat Kid: he must be behind me somewhere. There's a lot of chatter and giggling till slowly we realize the teacher is standing at the front, arms folded, waiting. She doesn't say a word, just stands there, her eyes traveling slowly along the rows of seated bodies. Gradually, it goes quiet. Someone shuffles their feet and someone else coughs and still she doesn't speak, till you realize it's so quiet you can hear the clock ticking. By now it's getting boring and still she stands there watching us.

"Thank you," she says at last, smiling. "I'm sure this is the first and last morning that you're going to take so long to settle yourselves."

There's a muffled giggle from somewhere, and everyone knows where because her eyes are now boring into a girl on the other side of the room.

"Could you share the joke with us?" she says, smiling.

There's no answer, and now everyone is sitting up straight and trying not to draw attention to themselves. I've got this sudden itch, right in the middle of my back, but I daren't move to scratch it.

"I am Ms. Benton," she announces, and writes it on the blackboard. "Pronounced MIZ Benton," she says, underlining the Ms. "And you are 8B." She writes that on the blackboard, too, and turns her eyes onto us again. "I am your tutor, not only for this year but also for the rest of your time at this school. That way we should get to know one another very well."

There's just the sound of the clock; I must have imagined the groan in my head.

"I teach Maths throughout the school, and no doubt I shall have the pleasure of seeing some of you in my year-eight maths set. As well as registration each

106

morning and afternoon in this room, and PSE of course, I am responsible for helping you with any worries or problems that you may have."

The way she's looking at us, I'm wondering if anyone would dare have a problem or a worry. And what's PSE?

"Or," she pauses and gives an extra-wide smile, "for reporting to your parents any worries or problems the school has about you."

Her eyes rest on some poor kid near the back who shuffles in his seat.

"Now," she says, "let's start getting to know one another, shall we?"

She picks up the register and makes each one of us stand up and sit down as she calls our names. Then she gives out the timetables. They may as well be in Martian, for all the sense they make. It's all in tiny, coded, computer print, and we stare at them, wondering what it all means. I look at Richard for help, but he's wearing his inscrutable expression: the one he's been fooling teachers with for years, that makes them think he's concentrating real hard when all the time he's wondering what his mum has packed him for his lunch.

I look for today, Thursday, but there isn't a Thursday, or a Friday, or any day of the week, come to that. Here's the mysterious PSE, but what's FT? So Ms. Benton spends the next half hour explaining about a ten-day week and how this is Day One and tomorrow is Day Two and PSE is Personal and Social Education and FT is Food Technology and what all the other little letters and codes mean and slowly it begins to sink in.

"Right," she says. "Let's see how much has penetrated into those brains of yours. Paula Jenks? Tell me, where will you be on Day Three in sessions four and five? Find Day Three, dear. That's right, put your finger on it, help her someone, now run your finger down till it's level with the figures four and five in the left margin. Now, Paula . . . ?"

"Maths, Mrs. Benton?" says Paula about five minutes after everyone else has worked it out.

"Miz," corrects Ms. Benton. "Well done. Now . . ." Her eyes scan the room for another victim. You have to stop yourself from ducking. "Richard Prescott—on what day will you need to bring your gym kit?"

"Day Three, next Monday?" says Richard.

"Excellent," she announces.

At last, satisfied that 8B is not going to be turning up for RE in football kit or for FT with their drawing pads, she lets us put the timetables away "in a safe place, as replacement copies from the school office will cost 10p each." Then she tells us that we won't be needing them till this afternoon anyway, as the morning is to be spent getting to know the school. It's nice to know that we lugged all our gear to school for nothing, as we've only got English and Geography this afternoon.

"Now," she says. "The back row—I never trust anyone who heads straight for the back row."

The rest of us, the ones that can be trusted, turn to give smug smiles at the back row. She's dead right. There's Dale Tranter and Stuart Flint shirking in the back row.

"So we'll have the back row out to the front, please, where I can see you properly."

And next she makes us all get up and rearrange ourselves, boy, girl, boy, girl, which is not easy as it's a bit cramped and we've all got bulging bags, but no one dares moan even when someone's stray bag makes me buckle at the knees.

"That's much better," she announces when at last we're all sorted out and everyone's looking dead miserable. But she hasn't finished yet.

"Good," she says. Then, still smiling, "And now, so that you can get to know one another properly, I want each of you to turn to the person sitting next to you and find out their names and something interesting about them."

We all give embarrassed glances at the person sitting next to us, but no one says anything. The girl next to me is more interested in the zipper on her pencil case.

"Go ahead, talk to one another," orders Miz.

A slow murmur starts to spread around the room.

"Well, then," says the girl next to me. "What's your name?" So I tell her, and she tells me she went to see *Joseph's Amazing Technicolor Dreamcoat* over the holidays and her name is Sarah Bradshaw.

But worse is to come, because Ms. Benton goes around and asks some of us to stand up and tell the rest what we've learned about each other. The girl next to Richard tells us that Richard likes chocolate, which is like saying vampires quite like blood, and that he enjoys poetry, which is news to me but you can see Miz is impressed.

At last the bell goes and we stumble out. I see Alex Moss go past with another boy whose name I can't remember. I'd almost forgotten about him. I feel brainwashed.

"Poetry?" I say when Richard comes out. "You like poetry?"

"I said pottery," said Richard. "She asked me what my favorite lesson was and I said pottery."

We follow everyone else to the playground and meet up with Simon and Jonathan. Jonathan boasts about how Mr. Gardener, his teacher, let them play handball all morning. Simon, whose class has been taken on a tour of the school, says he feels more confused than ever.

"Did you know that Richard likes poetry," I tell them.

"I said pottery!" Richard yells.

"I'm starving," says Jonathan.

"There's a snack shop in the hall," I tell them. I know this because Lucy helps with it sometimes.

"Did you notice," says Richard, as we head back after the bell, "how her eyes traveled along each row like one of those security cameras? I swear I could hear a whirr and click each time she scanned a face. She's probably got us all stored in her head on microfilm. I think she's a robot."

"She was smiling, though," I say. "Robots can't smile—they don't have a sense of humor, because it can't be programmed in."

"It wasn't a smile. It was a smirk," says Richard. "You could program a smirk. You just stretch the lips, like this."

He demonstrates a ghastly smile by stretching

his lips into a straight line. We're just climbing the steps up to our mobile when we get pushed from behind and the Longleat Kid and his friend rush past.

"Oi! Watch it!" says Richard.

"I hate that kid, I really hate that kid," I say.

"What? You know him?"

"Yeah. I know him. Unfortunately."

"Yeah? How come?"

But there's a sudden silence and we notice everyone settling into their seats and pretending to be busy. Miz is right behind us, so we hurry to our desks.

Ms. Benton hands out some more sheets, which tell us about all the school clubs and activities and which notice boards to look at for news about football or netball and how we must see Mr. Billings if we want to learn an instrument or join the orchestra. Then she spends a riveting ten minutes talking about Homework Diaries.

Alex Moss is just a couple of rows in front of me now, and I'm concentrating all my powers on the back of his neck when suddenly I get this pain in my shoulder blade that makes me turn round. It's Richard, behind me, prodding with a ruler.

"Why do you hate him, then?" he whispers.

But Ms. Laser Eyes has him pinned.

"Yes, Richard?" She smiles. "Did you want to ask something?"

"Er—I was just wondering—is there—er—a poetry club?"

After we've done our school tour, which, like Simon said, leaves you feeling even more confused, we have to rush off to get our lunch. We're on first sitting this week and we're late. You can hardly hear yourself think with all the clatter and chatter, and you have to think fast because the lunch ladies are moving you along so that everybody's out before second sitting.

Richard and me grab some pizza and beans and a drink and some chocolate slice and look out to the sea of faces for somewhere to sit. Then we see Jonathan and Simon across the hall, leaping up and down and waving their arms, so we head toward them. As we arrive, a lunch lady is ticking them off. "We don't expect that sort of behavior, you know. Does your mum let you leap up and down like that at home?" Only, she's having to shout to be heard.

As we tuck into our pizza we notice that Simon's got a baked potato and chips.

"You on a potato diet, then?" says Richard.

"No," says Simon. "This kid behind me kept telling me to hurry up. I couldn't think straight."

We discuss the morning's happenings, and Richard gives his impression of Ms. Benton's robot smile. Jonathan claims to be suffering from an overdose of Hangman because, apart from a quick tour round the school, they've been allowed to do what they like for the rest of the morning. I suggest they might be interested in the poetry club, which Ms. Benton is going to make inquiries about on Richard's behalf.

"That was your fault," says Richard. "You didn't have to make it so obvious when you turned round. Anyway, you still haven't explained why you hate that kid."

"What kid?" say Jonathan and Simon.

I look around the hall.

"That one over there," Richard points, "by the door."

"What, that big kid with the yellow hair?" says Jonathan.

"Yeah," I say, and they look at me, waiting for an explanation. I take a deep breath.

"His name is Alex Moss and his father is called Terence Moss. He's the man who killed Dad—the driver of the other car."

"What?" says Simon.

I don't know whether it's because he's checking if he heard right or whether he really didn't hear, because at that moment there's a great clatter as one of the dinner ladies pushes a loaded trolley past. So I'm shouting, "His father killed my dad!"

"So he got off?" says Simon. "Just walked away free? That's terrible. It shouldn't be allowed!"

"Yeah," says Jonathan. "It's terrible."

"My mum said she couldn't believe it when she read it in the paper," says Richard. "She rang your mum up and told her."

We're in the playground, leaning against the wall. No one says anything for a bit. That's why I don't like talking about it. No one ever knows what to say.

"How d'you know this Alex is his son, then?" says Richard after a bit.

"I've seen them, haven't I? I saw his father at the police station and I've seen them together loads of times."

Jonathan shakes his head and Simon stubs his heel against the wall behind.

"It's bad luck you being in the same class," says Simon. "When you think about it, the chances of that happening must be thousands to one."

What he's saying makes me think. Perhaps it's not bad luck. Perhaps it's all part of the pattern: another sign.

"I really, really hate him," I say.

"What's he like, then?" says Simon.

"Who? Alex Moss?"

"No, his father."

"He's a slob. He's got this great big belly and he's going bald. He drinks and lies around watching telly while his wife brings his meals on a tray. And he's had another accident with his car, as well."

"How'd you know all this?" says Richard.

"I know, right?" I yell, wishing I hadn't said so much. "So you'll just have to take my word for it!"

No one says anything for a while. Then Simon says, "Here—did I tell you about the ice creams you can get in France? There's this shop we went to where they had over a hundred different flavors—they were fantastic—I only managed thirty-two of them—but we're going again next year—Dad says . . ."

I make an excuse that I need the loo but it's more an excuse for getting away. I'm just coming out of the bathroom when Dale and Stuart pounce on me.

"Hey," says Stuart, "did we hear you right about someone killing your dad?"

"So what else is news?" I say. Everyone at our old school knew what had happened because Richard told me it was announced in assembly the day after.

"You know what he means," says Dale. "You were

shouting about it being some kid's father—some kid who was in the hall. We heard you."

"So?"

"So, who was it?"

I turn away, but as I do, who should be fooling around with his friend across the grass but Alex Moss.

"That kid over there," I say, nodding in his direction. "The one with the ball and yellow hair. Alex Moss."

Chapter 11

I can tell straightaway, the minute I walk into the classroom: something is different. It's the way everyone looks at me as I walk in: one girl nudges her friend and says something to her, and when I get to my seat a sort of hush falls, which I think must be because Ms. Benton has made her entrance, but when I look up it's the Longleat Kid and his friend, jabbering away as they come in, so they don't notice everyone's eyes on them. Then in come Stuart and Dale, looking pretty pleased with themselves, followed by Richard, who's late, and Ms. Benton. She calls the register, and all the while Sarah next to me keeps giving me the sort of look that Tom has when he watches that bit in the film when Bambi can't find his mother.

I guess what's happened. Now I know why Dale and Stuart were hanging around outside the mobile. It's confirmed when we make our way across to the English room. Sarah and her friend tag on to me and her friend says, "I think it's terrible that they've put you in the same class."

"What are you talking about?" I say, though I know.

"We know," says Sarah. "Everyone knows. About that Alex Moss's father killing your dad in a car crash. It must be terrible for you."

"Yeah, thanks."

Sarah gives her Bambi smile again.

It's English first, and after a brief talk by Mrs. Young, the teacher, we have to get into groups of four. She gives us some photos of different people and we have to write down the sort of things they might say. As we move into our groups, it's clear that no one is rushing to join Alex Moss and his friend, who I now know is called Rob, till finally Mrs. Young sorts it out. You can tell he's noticed, though, that something's going on. After a while, Mrs. Young collects all the photos and pins them to a board and each group has to read out what they've written and we have to guess which photo it might be. The first group says things like, "Who you staring at?" and "This is my dog Elvis," so it's not hard to guess that it's picture number three of a punk with spiky green hair holding a dog on a bit of string for a lead. The vicar is dead easy too. But the minute Dale says, "What I like best is driving real fast," and Stuart says, "Too bad if someone gets in my way—

that's their lookout" and the way they look over to Alex as they're saying it, everyone except Mrs. Young knows it's not really picture number one of a man standing by his car that they're talking about. But we go along with it.

"Well done," says Mrs. Young. "Some very imaginative ideas there."

"What's going on?" says Richard as we head for Geography.

"Don't look at me," I say.

"How come everyone seems to know, then?" he says.

"Dale and Stuart, I guess. They must have spread it around."

"What you tell them for? They're the last ones I'd tell anything. You didn't even tell me till today, and I'm supposed to be your friend."

"They heard," I say. "They overheard me telling you."

He lets out a long breath through his teeth, like a hiss.

"There's going to be trouble," he says.

"Perhaps there ought to be trouble," I say. "You said yourself it was terrible his father got away with it."

"Maybe," he says.

120

We file into the Geography room, and as everyone sits down you can see a big space around Alex and Rob. A couple of girls head for their row, but Dale jumps up and stands in the way.

"Excuse me, *please*, can you move?" says one of them. I think her name's Kim. But Dale folds his arms and says, "And who's going to make me?"

Then in comes the teacher, who says, "We can't have this gap in the middle. Come along—move forward."

So they move forward, but there's still a space by Alex.

"What is the matter with you?" says the teacher as they settle.

"There's a funny smell coming from somewhere, sir," says Dale.

Someone sniggers.

"That's quite enough," he says. "Someone give these books out, please."

He's right. It is enough. Enough for Alex Moss to get the message and take it home to his father.

"I don't like it," says Richard as we head for our bikes. "I'm not saying I'm not sympathetic like. I know how you must feel—"

"You don't know," I say. "Unless it's happened to

you, you don't know. And you don't have to like it either, because it's nothing to do with you."

I pedal off to Vic's to do my round.

As I cycle down the lane, past the back of thirty-six, I peer in, half expecting to see Alex Moss back home, kicking his ball around, but there's no sign of life. What I don't expect to see, ten minutes later, as I'm shoving the *Evening News* through the letter boxes of Abigail Road, is what's standing in the front of Longleat Man's garden. It wasn't there this morning: someone must have put it there today. Someone from Foster and Sykes Estate Agents, because it's their name on the big red and white For Sale sign that's sticking out above the hedge.

I stand there for a few minutes, taking it all in. I'm holding number thirty-four's paper ready, so I pretend to be delivering at thirty-six instead. I walk up the path and listen for a bit, just in case. But everything tells me there's no one home. I push the letter flap and peer in: I can see the *E.D.P.* still there, sticking out from a pile of letters and envelopes, and the free paper, the *Advertiser.* The sun is shining through the half-shut door at the end of the hall, making a triangle of light on the carpet. I'm pretty certain the door hasn't moved since this morning. I look in the front window: everything is neat and tidy. And the same when I go round the back and peer into the kitchen window. So what's going on? The For Sale notice has only just gone up, but it looks as if they've gone already. But they can't have; all their stuff's still here. Not just the furniture, but the dishcloth draped over the taps and a dirty coffee cup on the worktop. But all that Vic says when I ask him is that all the papers were canceled on Wednesday.

I take a ride back there at about eight, but nothing has changed: there's definitely no one there. So where have they gone? And why? They can't be far away, not if Alex Moss is at Colman High.

There's only one reason I can think of: I've won. He can't take the pressure; the Nightmare Plan has worked. He's gone into hiding, moved somewhere else. He got the message and he didn't like it.

But the funny thing is, I don't know how I feel about it. I should feel great, amazing even. But I don't, and I can't explain why.

Chapter 12

I had that dream again last night; the one where Dad's drifting away and I'm clinging to this tiny lump of ice. But what's worse is that this time, even when he's up close, I can't make out his face. It starts to fade and then it turns into Longleat Man's and then it fades again. And when I wake up I can't picture his face at all. The harder I try, the worse it is, so before I leave for the round I have to go into the sitting room and get the photo album from the bookcase. I'm staring down at Dad's face in a photo where all of us are sitting round the table at Christmas dinner at Auntie Jill's: Dad and Gran and Grandad, Lucy, Mum and Uncle John and the twins and Tom wearing the false mustache from his cracker and everyone with silly hats . . . I'm dreading Christmas.

I can hardly keep my eyes open in Maths this morning. I'm in a different set from Richard; it was never his strong point. I keep seeing the For Sale sign and wondering if I'm right about it. It nags at me like an ear-ache. Who's won, then? Him or me? If I'm right, and the plan has worked, shouldn't I feel different to the way I'm feeling now? Shouldn't I be feeling proud or something?

Someone's nudging me. I look up and see Kim, the girl next to me, holding out a bundle of worksheets; I take one and pass them along. THE MAGIC OF NUMBER, says the heading. So that's what Mr. Henderson's been talking about. Everyone's getting out pens and felt tips and looking purposeful.

"Come on, then," says Kim.

"Come on what?" I say.

"We're supposed to be working in pairs, right?"

"Right."

But it's difficult to concentrate. I keep seeing Alex Moss on the other side of the room; it seems we're in the same Maths set. And I know that what Simon said was right about the chances of us being in the same class and that there's a reason for it: that if Longleat Man has skived off, then A.M. is my link; a way of finding out where they've gone. What was it that Vic said? A Scorpio never lets go.

I stare sideways at him. "Your dad killed my dad," my head is saying, "and I'm not going to let him forget. Never. So you just take that message home."

He turns and sees me watching him. It's as if he's heard: he's looking at me hard, like he's challenging me. So I stare back, willing him to turn away first, like cats do.

The elbow nudges me again. "A great help you are," says Kim. "I may as well do this on my own. Are you helping or not?"

"Yeah, okay—sorry."

When I look back at A.M. he's looking at me over his shoulder, as if he's saying, "And who's going to make me, then?"

As we head out of Maths on to the long corridor that leads to the hall, I follow him toward the snack shop and watch him take his time in choosing some cookies and a packet of orange juice. I buy a can of Coke and follow him outside. He stands there, scanning the playground for his mate Rob, sucking his orange through his straw. I know he knows I'm watching him. Then he slowly turns toward me.

"I know what you want," he says. "You're after one of my signed photos—that's it, isn't it?"

I can't believe this. How can he make a joke of it? He knows by now that it was my dad that his dad killed.

"What's up?" says a voice next to me. It's Richard with Simon and Jonathan.

"He knows what's up," says Jonathan.

A.M. shrugs his shoulders, closes one eye, and, holding the empty juice packet between his finger and thumb, slowly aims it at the litter bin; it makes a perfect arc and disappears dead center.

I feel as if someone's wound a spring inside my head and it's straining to unwind.

He picks up his bag, puts his hand in his pocket, and starts to walk away. I step in front of him. "You know what's up," I say between my teeth. "Don't pretend you don't—your dad killed mine, and he got away with it! That's what's up!"

Dead calm, he drops his bag, puts both hands in his pockets, and takes a sudden interest in a patch of tarmac between his feet.

"And what am I supposed to do about it?" he says at last, looking up at me.

"You might at least sound sorry!" says Richard, looking a bit embarrassed; he always avoids confrontations.

"Yeah," says Jonathan. "The least you could do is apologize."

A.M. looks over to the roof of the Art block, looks down at his feet, slowly shakes his head, looks up, grins, and shrugs. "Okay—sorry. All better now?"

It's as if it's all one big joke to him.

"You might say it as if you meant it," says Richard. "It's his dad we're talking about, not a pet gerbil."

A.M. shrugs again with the palms of his hands held upward, picks up his bag, and turns away. I watch him as he takes a little run at an apple core that someone's dropped and kicks it across the playground into the bush by the path.

"Didn't you hear?" shouts Simon after him.

"Yeah, I heard," he says without turning round.

"He's a jerk!" says Jonathan, loudly enough for him to hear.

"A total nerd!" calls Simon.

Richard's looking at me.

"Thanks," I say.

It's all I can manage. Why couldn't it have been his dad that got killed? Why did it have to be mine?

It's Art after break. "Hi, troops," says the teacher, who introduces himself as Mr. Kaitzer. He tells us to get out our drawing pads and pencils, but three of the class have forgotten theirs and he disappears into his cupboard to sort something out.

A.M.'s one of them. He's tipping back on his chair and nattering away to his friend Rob, who suddenly starts to laugh. Then A.M. mutters something in his ear, and when they see me watching they both laugh.

"He makes me sick," says Richard, which is strong, coming from him. The other kids on our table are all ears: a couple of boys called James and Danny, and Nichola and Susan from our old school. James leans forward. "His dad really did kill your dad, then? How? What happened?"

So I tell them.

"It wouldn't be so bad if he acted as if he was sorry," says Richard, who goes on to tell them about the playground event.

I'm drawing spiky little bubbles around all the words on the cover of my pad so it looks as if they're all exploding.

"Right now, all you eager people," says Mr. Kaitzer, "let's get on. Now, who can tell me what this is?"

Only a couple of hands go up, because, like me probably, others are thinking it's a trick question as what he's pointing at on the table is a large ball.

"A ball?" says someone.

"Another name for a ball?" he demands, pointing at someone who is immediately struck dumb. Then someone says, "A sphere?"

"How do you know it's a sphere?"

"Because it's round," we tell him.

"How do you know it's round?" he says. "Look— this is round," he says, picking up a plate. "How do you know it's not a plate?"

"Because the plate is flat," says Nichola.

"And how do you know that the sphere's not flat?" he asks, till we're all staring at this ball and trying to work out how we know. Then he pulls down the blinds and starts to shine a torch on it from different angles so all the shadows shift about, and we start to understand what he's getting at. The next thing is he's put out lots of different shapes—cones and cubes and cylinders—and we're trying to draw them.

". . . so that I feel I can put my hand out and lift them from the page," he tells us.

By the time he gets round to me, I've made three attempts at the sphere and rubbed them all out because Richard said they looked like dirty snowballs.

"Bounce away, did it?" says Mr. Kaitzer. "Never mind—try again."

"Very good," he says to Richard. "Very good indeed."

I draw another ball, and next to it I draw two little figures, so that it looks like they're standing in the path of a huge boulder. One of them is bald and has a fat belly, and the other's a bit smaller and has strawlike hair. Their mouths are open in horror and their eyes are popping as I draw in little speed lines behind the boulder to show it's rolling toward them. Then I draw in a speech balloon coming from their mouths: "Help! Help!" they're yelling.

When the bell goes, I'm one of the first out.

"Hold on!" calls Richard. "Wait for me!"

"Can't!" I yell. "Got to do my paper round."

But what is really on my mind is keeping a tail on Alex Moss. I want to know where Longleat Man is living now. But even though I get to the bike shed in record time, by the time I've unlocked it there's a logjam trying to get through the gate. I see A.M.'s yellow hair disappear round the corner, and when I get out on to the road at last, he's gone.

As I pass number thirty-six with the last of the papers, the phone is ringing. It rings and rings, stops for a few seconds, then starts up again. Someone wants to buy his bargain Escort. But no one's answering.

The paper round seems to take hours. I'm wondering how I've kept both of them up for so long. I hate doing them now. And what's the point anymore? When I take my bag back to the shop I tell Vic I'm giving in my notice, making the excuse I'm getting too much homework. "You're not deserting me, too?" he jokes. But it turns out he's got a list of kids waiting for a round so I can finish now, this minute: just like that. As he sorts out the little bit he owes me, he's telling a customer about some story he's read of a woman who had a haunted fridge. "True as I'm standing here," he's saying. "She opens it up in the morning and there'd be these marks in the butter and things moved about and the milk all spilt—she lived alone, see, so she knew it couldn't be human, could it?"

I'm going to miss Vic.

When I get home, Mum's making a pot of tea and Tom is carefully arranging some cookies on a plate. This is unusual: we usually just grab them from the tin. Then, when he carefully carries them over to Matthew and politely offers them to him, I see why: in a circle of boring shortbread is one chocolate cookie. Matthew dives for it, and Tom is watching Matthew as his teeth sink into the rubber; then he takes it out, turns it over, and tries again. Tom is giggling his head off. "Got you!" he shouts, jumping up and down.

"Well," says Mum to me, "what did you do at school today?"

"Nothing."

There are horrible sounds coming from the door to the dining room. It's Lucy doing her clarinet practice.

I go into the sitting room, flop onto the sofa, and flick on the TV. It's like there's a great black hole sucking me down. Not the one Dad left, but the one left by Longleat Man. What am I going to do now? What's it going to be like without the Nightmare Plan? Perhaps I shouldn't have given the rounds up. How am I going to fill all that space?

Chapter 13

The stupid thing is, I'm awake by six o'clock this morning, Saturday, and I'm half dressed before I remember that I don't have the round anymore. And I've got a whole day to fill; no, a whole weekend. I feel really low and tired. I know it's something to do with the dream I had last night; one of those really frightening ones when you try to scream and nothing comes out. I don't remember the details: I blanked them out. You can do that, you know. The big mistake is to go over them in your mind and then you can't shake them off. All I remember is that it was a dream that I didn't want to remember, though I know it had Dad in it and Longleat Man.

I flop back onto the bed. I'll go over to thirty-six later and check it out again, then I could go along by the river for a bit.

"Joe? Are you all right, Joe?"

"What?"

It's Mum, looking down at me, holding an armful of ironing. I must have dozed off.

"What's the time?" I say.

"Nearly half past ten—you didn't deliver the papers wearing that, did you?"

"What?" I look down and see I'm wearing my pajama top and jeans. I sit up and rub my eyes.

"No—I didn't do it—I forgot that—"

"You forgot, Joe? Well, you'd better ring the shop straightaway and apologize. Say that you—"

"Mum—hold on! I don't mean I forgot. I chucked it—yesterday—both rounds, and Vic's got someone else now. But I'd started to get dressed before I remembered—I must have fallen asleep again."

I'm pulling off my top and reaching for my T-shirt.

"Well, I'm pleased to hear you've seen sense at last," says Mum, opening drawers and slipping stuff in. "But it would be nice if you'd told me yesterday, wouldn't it?" she says, turning to look at me. "And I'm wondering how many other things you haven't told me."

"Like what?" I say, glancing up at the top of my wardrobe where my diary's hidden underneath my big Construx set.

"Anything at all," says Mum, slamming a drawer. "It's not much to ask that you speak to some of us sometimes, is it, Joe? And hang your blazer up! No! Not on the chair—on a coat hanger!"

There's nothing new at thirty-six: a few more envelopes and some coupons on the mat, that's all. The back gate's been bolted; you can't get in that way anymore. I sneak through the side gate and check the back door and the windows, but everything's locked. I give up. As I leave, the phone starts ringing.

"Can't stay away, can he?" says Vic when I wander in.

"I was bored," I say.

"I wish someone would give me the chance to be bored," says Shirley, who's price-labeling a stack of sweets and chocolate bars.

"I could help—I've got nothing else to do."

"Here you are, then," says Vic, handing over a broom. "You can sweep up round the back."

After that, he gets me tidying up the magazines and taking down the out-of-date ad cards in the window, and then I help mark up the papers. It fills up some of the space—that and Vic's nonstop free advice and information service. I can hear him from the back of the shop: "Look—if they brought in a law that everyone had to have their fingerprints on record, on a computer, like, think how much time the police would save—they'd have copped whoever it was that broke into the shop last Christmas . . ."

I wake up to the sound of a horrible scream; it's not mine. It's coming from downstairs. Then it falls to a deep groan. It's Lucy practicing her clarinet again. I can't believe the time; it's nearly eleven. I can't remember when I slept so late. When I go down, the Sunday papers are on the kitchen table but there's no sign of life. Unless you count the noises coming from the dining room. It's different now, more like someone being tortured slowly.

I go into the sitting room with my Shreddies and flick the telly on.

"Oh no," moans Lucy when she comes in a few minutes later. "You're not going to be here, are you? Can't you go out? You're always out. Why do you have to be in today?"

"Then it's my turn to be in, isn't it? Anyway, what's it to you?"

"Some friends are coming round."

"Use your room, then."

"But we've got a video. It's all arranged."

"I've got a right to watch telly when I want. It doesn't belong to you, you know."

"Pig!"

"You have to learn to ask nicely," I tell her.

She flounces out.

"Where is everyone?" I shout.

"Out," she mutters when she comes back in and slides a video into the machine. "Look, you will disappear when they come, won't you? *Please!*"

"I'll think about it." I remember that's what Dad used to say.

"Well, don't take too long. They'll be here soon."

"Where have they gone, then?"

"Who?"

"Mum and Tom."

"Oh—some place, Holkham Hall or something, with Gran and Grandad."

There's a ring at the door and she goes to answer it, and I hear their shrieking voices and giggling in the hall.

"Excuse my brother," Lucy says. "He's just going."

I read through my diary, then I switch on my computer and play Zool for a bit, but I'm useless today. I could cycle to the river, but I feel too tired. I read the diary again, but I know it by heart now. I wander into Tom's room and check that he's taking proper care of my Junior Joker's kit; surprise, surprise, it's all there, though the cookie's got a few teeth marks on it now. I find my old hammer bench at the back of the cupboard; I'd forgotten all about that. You have to bang these little wooden pegs down a hole and they shoot out the other end, but it gets boring after a few goes.

Lucy and her friends are making enough noise: I can hear them every time the sitting-room door opens and they go chattering into the kitchen; in and out, in and out: it's driving me crazy.

I cross into Mum's room. It's not changed, not since B.T.A. All Dad's stuff just lying about; his reading glasses still by the bed. Without thinking, I open the wardrobe doors and stand there, just looking. His clothes are still hanging there, as if they're waiting for him to come back and fill them. And I still can't believe he won't; not really. I *know* he won't, but I can't believe it. Half the wardrobe's full of Mum's stuff; no, not half: more like two-thirds. But where hers is all crammed together and jumbled with piles of shoes spilling out, Dad's are all neat and tidy, just as he left them. Here's his old corduroy jacket and his denim shirt. I lift the sleeve of the jacket and press my face against it. But it doesn't smell of Dad anymore: it smells of Mum. And there's some of her makeup on the cuff.

Chapter 14

I never thought I'd ever be wishing the weekend away and eager for Monday. It's a relief this morning when all I have to do is put on my uniform and cycle off, knowing that my day is all filled up and planned out for me. But then things start to go wrong: first I get it in the neck from Ms. Benton because I hadn't remembered to get my stupid homework diary signed, and then, because I'd forgotten to do my Maths homework, I have to stay in at lunchtime and do it. I didn't mind that so much; I'm getting fed up with the "what-we-did-in-the-holidays" talk. But according to Richard, I missed all the excitement: some sort of scrap between A.M. and some other kid and it ended with apple pie and custard all over the kid's new blazer and A.M. gets sent off to the Head of Year. You should have seen him when he came back at registration. He looked just like those times I saw him with Longleat Man. Even Ms. Benton's penetrating stare didn't have any effect; he just slid down in his seat with his arms folded and stared out the window.

I've been watching the clock, waiting for the final bell to go, because I've decided that, whatever happens, I'm going to find out where Longleat Man is. I'll leave my bike in the bike shed—I can always come back for it—and I'll trail A.M. home. It goes like a dream, because there are so many kids crowding out onto the pavement that he can't see me even if he does turn round. Then the next minute, just as we get round the corner, him and Rob start to run and they've hopped onto the bus that's just moving off from the stop. And all I see is A.M.'s legs disappearing up the stairs.

"I forgot to tell you," says Mum at breakfast. "You've got an appointment at the dentist's this morning—I found the card behind the tea caddy. Good job I noticed it."

"When?"

"Nine o'clock."

"I'll be late for school."

"It's only a checkup—you won't be that late. I'll write you a note."

"You never made appointments in school time before—even when I asked so that I could miss French."

"I got the weeks mixed up. I thought school started *this* Thursday."

I look at the wall calendar; it's still on February. It's like everything came to a stop when Dad went.

Mum's right: I'm not that late, but I've got to have a filling—next Wednesday at nine-fifteen. My class is still in year-eight assembly, but I've missed registration so I have to go to the office. "Thank you, dear," says the school secretary. "Pop your note in the register and bring it here, will you, so that I can mark you in? Year eights are over there on the left."

I find 8B's register and open it up. I've never really seen inside a class register before; never realized that next to the column of names, hidden under the narrow sheet where the rows of little red V's stretch across in zigzags, are all our addresses. I never thought it could be this easy. Here's Alex Moss's: "36 Abigail Road" has been neatly crossed out, and over the top is written "2D Heron House, Chantry Road, Norwich."

It's not what I expected: a big, square-looking building just past the fish-and-chip shop, about a five-minute bike ride from school. I looked it up in Mum's *A-Z*. There's no garden, just a walled-off area at the back with car parking spaces, a line of dumpsters, and a fenced space with washing lines and garbage cans. All the cans and the car spaces have white numbers painted on them. There's nothing parked where it says 2D. I leave my bike behind the fence out of sight; I don't want to lock it in case I have to make a quick getaway. I'm feeling tight, wound-up like, in case I botch it, or worse, not find out what I need to know. And what if I run into A.M.? Or both of them? Don't think about it.

There are double doors at the front with wired glass panels, and the paint's all peeling. I can see there's no one about, so I push the doors and go in. It's a bit dark, but I can see some steps ahead and there are corridors off to each side and signs with arrows saying *Flats 1A–1D*, and *Flats 1E–1H*. Just inside the door there are these little cupboards with slits at the front of each and numbers painted on them; letter boxes, I suppose. Someone's scrawled "Wayne Loves Himself" across them in black marker. I make my way toward the stairs and see a sign pointing up: *Flats 2A–2H* and *Flats 3A–3H*. I'm standing with one foot on the step, checking that it's clear to go up, when I hear the swish of the doors behind me, and when I look there's this old lady with frizzy orange hair coming through, more interested in her handbag than in me. Then, as she pulls out a key, she sees me.

"Looking for someone, are you?"

"Er, yes—Mr. and Mrs. Moss."

She stares at me as if I'm up to no good.

"Got the wrong place, then, haven't you? No one here called Moss. Go on, clear off. We're fed up with you kids coming in here and leaving your cans and chip papers and worse lying around."

"No, it's 2D I'm looking for—they've just moved in," I say.

She walks toward me and waves her keys at me as she says, "I've told you there's no one here called Moss. I've lived here for five years—it's Mr. and Mrs. Parker at 2D. Go on, clear off—before I fetch my husband.

She stands and watches as I leave.

I go out of the door and round the corner, count up to a hundred, and then, after a quick glance inside, push through the doors and make a dash for the stairs. *Flats 2A–2D,* says a sign pointing to the right. 2D's right down at the end. And below the doorbell, written on a bit of card held by a little metal frame, it says PARKER.

I couldn't take the risk, could I? What if I'd pressed the bell and it *was* them? What would I say? He might remember me and make a connection and it would be good-bye to the Nightmare Plan, for certain. Any other place I could have nipped off quickly and crouched behind the hedge or something and watched to see who opened the door, but you can't do that in a narrow corridor.

I don't go straight home, just ride around for a bit, not sure where, trying to think. I notice I must be going round in circles; I've passed that house with the fishing gnomes in the front garden before. My head's going round in circles too. There *is* something I could do, though. I head for Kwick Dry Cleaners. But even though I hang around for nearly ten minutes, there's no sign of Longleat Woman. And there's no red Escort in its usual place at Nelson's Print Works.

I've cycled miles and gotten nowhere. I'm nearly home before it hits me that there's one more thing I could try.

"Directory Inquiries—which town do you require, please?" says a woman's voice.

"Er—Norwich."

"Name and address, please."

"Parker, 2D Heron House, Chantry Road."

Then there's a click and a different voice says, "The number you require is Norwich . . ."

I repeat it in my head so I don't forget it, replace the receiver, and search in my pockets, panicking a bit in case I haven't got enough. But it's okay; I've got a 20p. I feed it into the slot and press the number out. It seems to ring for ages; then a voice says, "Hello."

"Is that Mrs. Moss?" I say.

"No . . ." The voice pauses. "Who is that?"

"This is one of Alex's friends . . ."

"Oh, I see. No—Alex isn't here at the moment. He'll be back for his supper, though—about six. Shall I say who called?"

"No, it's all right, thanks."

Chapter 15

You can't watch a flat, not like you can watch a house; you've got no cover. I've gone past the building a few times, but there's no sign of them. So where are they, then? Are they staying there, or what? And there's still no sign of them at Nelson's or the dry cleaning shop. I turn it over and over, trying to work it out.

Danny's giving out the English books. Mine flops onto the table and I open it up. There's a lot of red pen: *This is not good enough! Date? Title? See me.* I make my way out to Mrs. Young's desk and nod and shake my head in all the right places. No, I'm not proud of this work. Yes, I will make more effort. Yes, please, Mrs. Young, I would love to do it all over again for homework tonight.

As I head back to my desk, I can't help noticing how the class has arranged itself; it's the same every lesson now. Kim and her friend Laura have taken to sitting with Alex and Rob all the time. They were at the same school or something and they always keep to themselves, on the other side of the classroom from me and Richard. And Sarah, Nichola, Danny, James, and a couple of others, we all sit on the other side. Then there's Dale and Stuart, usually at the back, if they can get away with it, or trying to stir things up by sitting right behind Alex's group. And, of course, there are the neutrals, the ones who just keep their eyes down if something's going on, who fill the spaces in between.

It's just the same at break and lunchtimes and in group work, like drama. We had a long lecture from Ms. Benton this week, how we're getting a reputation for being the most uncooperative class in Year Eight, blah, blah, blah.

Things have started to go missing too. There was a big fuss on Monday when James reported that his lunch money had gone missing. Then yesterday Alex Moss says someone's stole his trainers from his gym bag, so this massive search is organized and Mr. Gardener makes everyone turn out their bags and James's empty wallet is found in Alex's bag. The Head of Year must be sick of the sight of Alex Moss.

By time we'd missed most of PE. I'm just coming out of the loo when someone grabs me from behind, round the neck. It must be Rob, because Alex Moss is there grinning at me, leaning against the sink with his hands in his pockets. Then he has the nerve to say, "You're in big trouble—you know that? Because I've just about had enough of you, so I'm giving you a warning—lay off!" He walks over and shoves his face right up to mine. "Get the message? And this is to remind you," he says, and he takes out a pair of scissors. He grabs me by the tie and cuts it off, leaving just this little bit dangling, and stuffs the bit he's cut off in my top pocket. Then Rob says, "I think he needs a haircut, don't you?" and while he's holding me round the neck, A.M. is going snip, snip over my head, while I'm wriggling and kicking. Then a couple of year tens come in, and they let go, strolling out as if nothing's happened. I hate him. I really hate him.

"This is crazy," says Richard when I tell him. "He's mad. You've got to tell someone. Tell your mum and get her to ring the school. They could move him to another class or something—another school even."

"I'll think about it," I say.

I'm cycling back from my appointment at the dentist, one side of my mouth numb and my tongue all thick, but I don't go to school. I head off toward Chantry Road instead. I'm going to risk it. It's the only time I

149

can be sure A.M.'s not going to be in. And if it is Longleat Man, I'll just pretend I got the wrong flat.

I take a deep breath and press the bell above the PARKER label and make myself wait. There's the sound of movement inside and the door opens.

"Yes?"

It's an old lady, and behind her, through an open door, I can see an old man in an armchair, and hear the sounds of the television.

"I brought this," I say, pulling a letter from my pocket. It's a letter that Mum got yesterday and threw in the garbage; a catalogue for thermal underwear or something. I've stuck a label over the front and written "Mr. and Mrs. Moss, 36 Abigail Road," but I've deliberately smudged the six.

"I'm from number thirty-eight," I say. "This came to our house by mistake. Mum said she'd heard they'd moved here and asked me to drop it in on my way back from the dentist."

"No, they're not here," she says, turning it over and examining it. "But I'll send it on. Thanks anyway."

And she closes the door.

Chapter 16

So they've gone away. I've won. But every time I see Alex Moss, I remember. You can't forget him. Anytime there's trouble, he's there, at the center of it, pretending it's nothing to do with him, shrugging his shoulders with that "don't blame me" look. And all that showing off he does with his trick footwork in football and Mr. Gardener always going on about it: "Right, Alex, just give us a demonstration, will you, so the others can see what you can achieve with practice."

"Mmmm, very nice," A.M. says to me when I turn up wearing my new tie that I had to buy with my own money so that Mum doesn't ask awkward questions.

"Bit long, though—how about I trim it a bit?" Then he laughs and walks away. "Anytime," he says, walking backward. "Just say—I do haircuts as well—snip, snip."

It's when we're in the changing rooms after Games at the end of the afternoon that things really begin to happen. Half the year group have Games together, and Simon and Jonathan are in the same group as me and Richard. And probably nothing would have happened if Mr. Gardener, the teacher, had been there, but he had to go off for a few minutes to the office with a kid who accidentally got hit in the eye. So here we all are, shuffling in and out of the showers through the steam, when above the hubbub of kids shouting, "Yikes—it's gone cold!" and suchlike, someone shouts, "Right! Who's got them, then?"

It's Rob, A.M.'s sidekick. But they're both standing there with their towels wrapped round them, looking at me.

"I asked who's got them!" yells Rob, who's making sure everyone can hear, and looking over in my direction. "Someone's taken Alex's things and they're going to give them back!"

By now everyone's paying attention. Then he marches up to me, bare feet and just his towel, and starts going through my stuff, throwing my shirt and trousers into a horrible, slimy muddy patch made by my boots.

"Hey, watch it!" I yell. "Get off, will you?" and I'm trying to push him off.

Then he turns and sees Dale and Stuart, who can hardly contain themselves, and the smirks on their faces tell me they know more about what's going on than I do.

"It's you two, isn't it?" he yells.

"Yeah, I think so," says Dale. "I'll just check in the mirror." He gives a quick look at the mirror over the sink. "Yeah, it's definitely me and he's definitely Stuart. The real thing," he says, grinning.

"You know what I mean!" shouts Rob. "What have you done with Alex's stuff?"

"Search me," says Stuart. "Perhaps they accidentally got dropped in one of the bogs. I think I might have seen something in one of them, don't you, Dale?"

By now they're performing for the audience of kids who are changing silently or have stopped to watch, listening to every word and glancing over to Alex Moss, who's sitting there on the bench. He's looking at me hard, as if it's all my doing. I'm in the dark as much as anyone, but it doesn't stop me from getting a kick out of seeing him looking like an idiot.

A couple of kids have started banging doors into the cubicles and looking down the pans, then someone shouts, "Ugh! Is this what you're looking for?" and a whole crowd of boys surge forward to have a look: jostling and pushing, like it's the crown jewels or something. When we get to peer in ourselves, there's a pair of underpants down one loo and socks in another and his shirt is stuffed in the urinal.

But while all of this is going on, A.M.'s started to pretend he couldn't care less. While everyone else has been jostling past and making silly jokes, he's putting on his trousers and is now slipping his blazer over his muddy football shirt. He slips his bare feet into his shoes, looks at me, marches into the cubicle, and we hear the flush go. "Never liked them anyway," he says with a shrug as he comes out, and he gets a laugh. He doesn't even look bothered anymore, though you can't say the same for Rob, who's angrily stuffing his kit into his bag and glaring over at Dale and Stuart.

Then A.M. looks at me and Dale and Stuart and says, "Just tell me, then: who's the trainer and who are the monkeys?"

"Who are you calling monkeys?" says Stuart. "Did you hear, Dale? He's calling us monkeys."

"I just asked the question," says A.M. "You gave

the answer. Come on, Rob," he says, throwing his bag over his shoulder. Then he stops as if he's just remembered something and goes back into one of the cubicles, coming out with a pair of dripping boxer shorts, but you don't see them till he brings his hand from behind his back and flings them across the room and they land neatly on Dale's head.

The laughter bounces off the walls.

"He's really asking for it now," mutters Simon.

But Richard is wearing his inscrutable look.

"You're dead!" shouts Dale, flinging them back at him but missing. "Just you wait! You're dead!"

A.M. makes his hand into the shape of a gun with two fingers sticking out like a barrel and points it at Dale and Stuart. "Bang, bang," he says. Then he points them at me and opens and shuts his fingers like a pair of scissors. "Snip, snip," he says.

The bell goes and he's first out of the door just as Mr. Gardener comes in.

"What's all this?" he says. "Aren't you lot out yet? And I don't want anything left behind. What's that on the floor? You—pick them up. Anyone's? No? Who's gone home without his knickers, then? Right, when you're ready, take them to Lost Property. Hurry up, now."

And Stuart's left holding the boxer shorts, looking like he could commit murder.

"What was *that* all about?" says someone.

I walk to the bike shed with Richard. Jonathan and Simon stay behind for badminton club. Richard's acting inscrutable again.

"It's all out of control," he says. "It's going to get worse and worse. There'll be big trouble, you see."

"He deserves everything he's got coming."

"Yeah, but it's not just him, is it?" he says.

"Look—what's spooking you? You're not scared, are you?"

We've reached the bikes; most of the others have gone. I had to try and get that mud off my shirt and trousers, and it's made us late.

"I'll forget you said that," he says, strapping his bag to his bike.

"Look—can't you see—" He stops and looks at me. "Dale and Stuart are just as bad—they just like stirring it. They're just using you. What's going to happen next? Honestly, you ought to tell someone—before it's too late."

"You can't be serious!" I yell. "You know what he's like. He thinks—he thinks that Dad being killed was a big joke! Serves him right—I wish they'd shoved *him* down the bog and flushed it!"

"All I'm trying to say is—"

"Don't bother!" I say. "You made yourself perfectly clear!"

"Just listen, will you—"

I leave him standing there.

I arrive just in time for Friday morning registration. I don't even look at Richard. As days go, today is quiet; nothing goes missing. I avoid Richard and the rest and spend the breaks in the library. I've got to do all my maths again. "You do not appear to understand" is printed on the bottom of my page. And when I go to see Mr. Henderson he asks if perhaps I'd like to move down a Maths set if, like, if I'm finding the work a bit demanding in the top set. "But it's my best subject," I tell him. "That's as may be," he says.

I hang about in the cloakroom at the end of school, collecting my gear, mainly to avoid the traitor, Richard. Then I make my way slowly to the bike shed, but Richard is waiting. I ignore him, but he comes over.

"Get lost!" I say.

"What's happened to you?" he says. "I don't recognize you anymore! You know that! And what was all that 'I'm busy' stuff in the holidays?"

"Good," I say. "Then perhaps you'll leave me alone. I don't need you—I don't need anyone. That's something I've learned—without any help from you!"

"Okay," he says. "If that's the way you want it. I just hope no one gets hurt!"

"Yeah, well, I do! I hope that Alex Moss gets everything that's coming to him!"

"Get real, will you?" he shouts.

I turn away and strap my bag onto my bike.

"Okay," he says, getting on his bike. "Do what you like, but I don't want any part of it."

I wait for him to disappear then start to follow, but I don't feel like going home, so I turn back and head for the other exit out of school; I might call in at Vic's and give number thirty-six another look over. I'm just scooting past the kitchens when I hear some funny noises coming from behind the wall where the trash cans are kept: voices and scrabbling sounds. I peer through the open brickwork, but I can't see properly so I lay down my bike and reposition myself. It's Dale I see first, and he's grinning at something low on the ground so I have to move down the other end as the cans are blocking my view. As soon as I see the yellow hair, I know who it is on the ground. You can't see much else of him. Two big kids, year elevens at least, are on top of him, sitting on him, facedown: one on his shoulders and the other on his legs; and the one on his legs has pushed A.M.'s arm right up his back in a half nelson and he's bending back one of his fingers.

"We can't hear you," he's saying. "You've got to do better than that—we don't like people who aren't nice to my little brother. Now, I want a nice big 'sorry'—go on, say it: 'I'm very, very sorry, Dale, for chucking my smelly, disgusting underpants at you.' "

But A.M.'s not saying anything. I can't see his face; it's turned away.

"Still can't hear you," says Dale's brother, pulling hard on the finger.

"Okay, okay," comes a croak from A.M. "I'm sorry."

"I don't think he heard—did you, Dale?" he says. "And you didn't say it properly. So let's try again, shall we?"

He's pulling so hard on the finger, I think that it's going to snap soon.

So A.M. says the lot—at least I think he does, he's not speaking very clearly.

"Now beg for mercy," says the other kid, sitting on

his shoulders. "Go on—beg! Beg!" And the three of them start to chant, "Beg! Beg! Beg!"

But this time, when A.M. croaks back his answer, it sounds like "I think I ought to warn you—I'm a black belt in judo."

"Oh, a joker," says Dale's brother, and gives the finger an extra wrench, and you can see Alex's head twist and his feet jerk.

Before I know what I'm doing, I'm round to the other side of the wall, and they jump back, surprised to see me.

"Quick!" I'm yelling. "There's someone coming— Mr. Ray, I think."

They disappear as if they've never been there.

Slowly, painfully, A.M. levers himself up into a sitting position, his head bent over the hand he's cradling in his lap. When he looks up, his face is white and glistening, like it's been sprayed with water. After a bit I say, "Shall I get someone?"

"I thought someone was coming," he mutters, holding his head in his other hand.

"I made it up."

I'm trying not to see his finger, which is hanging at a strange angle. I don't know how long I stand there, looking at him. At last, he pushes himself up, leans against the wall, then, giving one last look at me, picks up his bag and walks away.

What a total creep, I'm thinking. I must be. Or else I'd have let them get on with it.

Chapter 17

A.M. wasn't at school yesterday, or today, Tuesday. Dale and Stuart have been swaggering about a bit more than usual, but Rob just keeps to himself, when he's not giving me black looks. And when Miz looks up in registration and asks him if he knows why Alex is away, he just shrugs and then narrows his eyes at me. I keep away from Richard and the rest and at lunchtimes disappear on my bike somewhere and buy chips or something: I prefer my own company. I haven't even been to Vic's, not for ages.

Wednesday morning and I'm pedaling the same old route to school when, for some reason, I find myself at the corner of Abigail Road. This is stupid, I'm telling myself. What am I doing here? I can see thirty-six easily, even from this far off, by the red and white sign that's sticking up from the hedge. Then I see someone coming out of the alleyway; someone with yellow hair and a blue blazer and carrying a rucksack.

162

If it's not Alex Moss, then it's his double. He vanishes out of sight, so I dash for the alleyway and race to the back fence.

I was right. It's him; he's in the garden. He's taken off his rucksack and his blazer and dumped them by the back door. Now he's bending over his bag, and when he stands up he's holding a football and I can see his hand is all bandaged up. He tosses the ball up and catches it on his head, gives it a few bounces, then lets it drop. He catches it on the bounce with his foot and starts to dribble it around the garden, stopping every now and then to do a bit more fancy footwork: onto his foot again, up to his knee, knee to knee, and then onto his head again. He must be skiving off.

I make it to school, but only just in time, and I'm wondering why I bothered. At lunchtime I cycle back there, but there's no sign of him, or after school when I check again.

If I'm right and he *is* skiving off, then he's going to be there the same time this morning too, so I wait on the corner of Abigail and congratulate myself when a minute or so later I see him come out of the alley and disappear into thirty-six. It's the same routine, and this time I stay to watch. I hate admitting it, but he *is* good:

the way he can control the ball on a foot or a knee or his head.

I check my watch: quarter past nine. Registration was twenty minutes ago. Who cares? I have to duck down and pretend to be examining the tire on my bike when a man walking his dog strolls past, and when I peer in again A.M.'s made himself well at home. He's dragged out the garden table and a chair and he's sitting with his feet up drinking from a can. This is boring, so I ride up the lane and back again. Now he's standing in the middle of the lawn and he's tossing balls into the air; but they're not balls exactly, more like soft cubes, three of them, juggling them into the air. It looks dead easy to me; it must be if he can do it with a hand bandaged. Then he stops, strolls around for a bit, and starts up again, only this time, after a minute or so, he lets one of the balls drop, catches it neatly on his foot, and kicks it up, but it goes wrong and they go all over the place. He tries again, and again, and each time they go flying, till suddenly he gets it right. One minute the little square bags are cascading in the air, then he pauses, drops one, flicks it up and they join the others rising and falling, over and over, and he repeats the throw, throw, drop, kick trick.

By now, my neck's a bit stiff and I need to check my tire again as a woman with a baby carriage pushes past, and when I look next he's walking toward the house. He bends down by one of the plant tubs, dead from neglect by the look of it, straightens up, and makes his way to the back door. Next minute, A.M., rucksack and all, has disappeared inside.

It's not worth going to school; it's nearly lunchtime anyway. I buy some chips and spend the rest of the day by the river.

I can't keep away. I know it's stupid, but I need to come. But this morning he doesn't turn up. I hang around till nine, then go round the back to check, but by twenty past it's clear he's not coming. I've missed school anyway, so what have I got to lose? I go round the side, taking my bike with me. The back door's locked but the key is under the plant tub, so I know for sure he's not here. The next minute, I'm standing in Longleat Man's kitchen. This is where the man who killed Dad slurped his tea and filled his fat belly.

I dump my bag and stand there, taking it all in. There's a funny smell coming from somewhere; something's definitely going off. I wander around, opening cupboards. It's dead weird: everything's still here: jams, tomato sauce, tins, sugar bowl. It's like Longleat Man and his wife have just been beamed away or something. The funny smell is coming from the grungy-looking cloth in the sink; it was hanging over the taps when I looked in a few weeks ago, so perhaps A.M.'s been coming here all the time and I never noticed. There are dirty mugs on the workshop too, and a plate, a knife with jam on, and some greasy chip paper.

I go into the hall; the stuff on the mat's still there and no one's touched it. I wander into the sitting room and I remember all the times I looked in from outside. I'm standing right by Longleat Man's armchair, where I watched him slumped in front of the telly. It all seems so ordinary: the music center, the magazines on the table, the bookshelves; they've even got *The A.A. Book of the British Countryside,* just the same as ours at home. The plant in the corner has definitely had it, though. And on top of the TV is a school photo of Alex Moss himself, smiling smugly at me.

I head up the stairs and peer through the doors. This must be his room: I can see the juggling bags on the bed. He's a Norwich City fan, no mistake: team colors, green and yellow, everywhere. Signed photos of Robert Fleck, Brian Gunn, Mark Robins; posters, score charts, rosettes, flags; you can hardly see the walls, and over the table a huge inflatable yellow canary. He's got a beanbag chair; I've always wanted a beanbag chair. I flop into it and get comfortable, studying the shelves;

166

all the usual stuff: Monopoly, Cluedo, Space Lego, boxes of tapes, *Beano* annuals, some Terry Pratchett books, and if I'm not mistaken . . . I get up and take a closer look. I'm right; a stack of Mr. Men books. I've still got mine too.

I get up and wander over to the bed and pick up the juggling bags; I've been dying to have a go at this. How did he do it, now? Two bags in one hand, one in the other—toss up, one two . . . whoops! Try again. One, two, three . . . whoa! They go all over the place and I have to go round the other side of the bed to pick them up. It's only when I'm getting up that I see Alex Moss standing in the doorway.

I don't think; just charge for the door. I don't remember what happens next, but somehow we end up on the floor. And we're rolling over and over and I'm kicking and yelling and trying to hit him with everything I've got: lashing out with feet, fists, knees, head. He's not going to beat me! I'm not going to let him beat me! I close my eyes and concentrate all my energy into pushing him off. I can hear grunting noises, like a wild animal, then I realize it's me. But it's no good! I can't do any more. When I open my eyes, I'm on my back and A.M. is sitting on top of me, pinning my shoulders down with his knees, and he's got both my arms stretched up above my head. He's looking at me like he hates me, and I turn my head away; I don't want to see what he's going to do next.

But he doesn't do anything. I can hear his heavy breathing and I'm panting too. Then, suddenly, he lets go and climbs off. He walks slowly to the bed, picks up the bags, and starts to juggle, over and over and over. He doesn't even look at me. I start to get up.

"It was you," he says. "Wasn't it? All that stuff you sent? The 'This car kills' bit?"

He's stopped now and he's watching me.

"I had to, didn't I? He killed Dad! It'd have been different if he'd been punished—but they let him off. He should have been put away—he would have been if it'd been a gun or a knife and not a car! Someone had to do something! He had to be reminded!"

"You haven't got a clue, have you?" he says slowly. "You make me sick—you know that?"

"I make *you* sick? You weren't even sorry! You stood in the playground like—like it was one big joke or something. If you at least *sounded* sorry . . . !"

"Me—sorry? I'm sick of being sorry—sick of apologizing for my father. I'm sick of the whole thing!" He's yelling now. "I mean—I don't believe this! What are you doing here anyway? This is *our* house! Are you crazy or something? What is it with you? You're really,

168

really sick—you know that? You send photos and chocolates and maniac messages till my mum's ill with worry! You set me up at school—till everyone's nudging and saying 'Is it true your father's murdered someone?'! You arrange this . . . !" He waves his bandaged hand at me. "And I'm supposed to say sorry?"

He throws his juggling bags across the room and the yellow canary goes swinging wildly on its cord.

"It wasn't like that!" I shout. "I had nothing to do with any of that!"

"No? Oh, no—you just spread the word around and stand back and watch—'His father killed my daddy!' and everyone's saying 'Oh, poor little Joe—let's get Alex, then!' Only, you forgot one little thing—he was found NOT GUILTY! Remember? Just a tiny detail you and everyone else seems to have forgotten!"

"Oh yeah? That's supposed to make it all right, is it? How come your lunatic father's car was on the wrong side of the road, then? And my dad ends up smashed into a telegraph pole? How come . . ."

But the words get stuck. I feel as if I'm choking and I can feel my face growing wet. Alex is staring at me, and I turn away. I don't want him to see me like this. No one's seen me like this. Not even Mum. Not even on Accident Sunday when the police brought her home. No one's seen me blub. But I know it's too late and I can't stop, so I head for the door. But then Alex says something, not yelling now.

"It wasn't his fault, right? He was on the wrong side because he'd swerved—because some idiot on a motorbike shot out, which you must know if you know so much about it."

"What?"

He's staring at me, like he's trying to read my thoughts.

"I don't believe you," I say.

He turns away and goes to retrieve his juggling bags.

"You're lying," I say. "You're making it all up!"

But he doesn't answer, just stands there, looking at me.

Then, slowly, he starts to toss the bags into the air, as if I'm not there.

Chapter 18

"Mum."

"Mmmm?" She's sitting at the dining-room table, sorting through letters and bills.

"You know the court case—about Dad? Why was he found not guilty?"

She gives me a quick glance and returns to a letter. "He said he was forced to swerve to avoid a motor-bike."

"But he made that up, didn't he?"

She doesn't look at me but straight ahead at the blank wall. "Well . . ."

"I mean—the police couldn't have believed him, could they? They wouldn't have charged him other-wise. He was telling lies, wasn't he, Mum? He got away with it, didn't he?"

She puts her pen down, turns to me, and breathes a long sigh. "There wasn't any evidence, Joe—not to begin with. But there was a witness—she didn't come forward straightaway—and there were some children who heard a bike . . ."

"But none of that was in the paper—you should have let me come! Why didn't you let me—?"

"Look, Joe, we've been through all this before," she says, pushing her hair back.

"But you said—you said you hated him—the other driver!"

"Oh, Joe," she says, leaning her head into her hands and staring down at the table. "Come here."

I go over to her. "Of course I hated him. I needed to hold someone responsible—it all seemed so senseless. . . ."

She stands up and wraps her arms around me.

"All I could think of was, why couldn't it have been him, not your dad? Why couldn't he have controlled his car properly? Surely he could have done *something* to avoid the accident? And then, when he was standing there in the court, as large as life—while your dad was . . . well, of course I hated him."

"Do you still hate him, then?"

"No—not really. How can I? I think it *was* an accident, Joe—they happen every day. I really don't think it was his fault, not anymore."

"But it might have been mine," I say. Only the words come out in a splutter.

"Of course not," Mum's saying. "How can it have been your fault, Joe?"

She steps back to look at me, and I can't stop.

"Well, you know that morning—when he went off? I'd left my bike on the drive—you remember he was always telling me off about it? And he called for me to come and move it so that he could back out of the garage—but I was busy. I was playing on my computer, so I pretended—I pretended not to hear. But I could see him from my window—he had to get out of the car and move it himself. If he hadn't had to do that—he wouldn't have been killed, would he? Those few minutes would have made all the difference! Can't you see? He'd have been on his way home—alive! Can't you see, Mum?"

I can feel my face out of control, all screwed up.

"Joe! Joe!" she's shouting at me and holding my head in her hands. "Listen to me, Joe! Joe! It was *not* your fault! You understand? Is that what you've been thinking? All this time? Oh, Joe," she's saying, "you've been the strong one! You seemed to deal with all of it so much better than any of us. It was Tom and Lucy I was more worried about. Lucy so tired and shutting herself away and Tom coming into my bed every night. Why didn't you tell me all this before?"

She bends down and looks at me.

173

"It's true that I was worried when you spent so much time away. But I thought that it was just your way of coping, especially when you said you'd found a friend who didn't know about Dad. You can't imagine how terrible I felt when you gave me your paper-round money. You've always been the one I could rely on, Joe—the steady one. You know, you're so much like your father, Joe . . ."

"Why did he do it?" I say.

"Who, Joe?"

"Dad. Why did he leave us, Mum? Why did he go and get killed? He was supposed to be invincible."

Later, after supper, I slip out. I cycle to the river and stand on the bank, watching the red cover of the diary disappear out of sight beneath the smooth, green water.

As I cycle back, it's already dusk and the streetlights are coming on. I can see the lights of our house glowing in the distance. It feels good to be going home.

Chapter 19

Monday and Alex still isn't here; a whole week he's been skiving off. I'm not sure I'm here myself. Mrs. Hickmott is showing us how to keep a kitchen free from germs, but I keep seeing Alex Moss, even though he's not here. I don't think I hate him anymore, which makes it worse. It was less complicated when I did. Now I've got to try and think what to do next. But my head's so full, there's no more room: I've reached overload. Every time I try to think, it's like little flashing words keep coming up: error; disk full.

But I know I must be here when at lunchtime Ms. Benton taps me on the shoulder and asks me to stay behind for a few minutes. She waits for everyone to leave, pulls a chair up to her desk, and nods for me to sit down. Then she picks up her pen and starts to roll it between her fingers.

"I'm a little concerned about you, Joe—for a number of reasons. First of all . . ." She leans back in her

chair and taps her pencil on the folder in front of her.
". . . because of the reports I'm receiving from other
teachers about your work."

She looks at me. "It doesn't match with the com-
ments I have here from your last school."

She leans forward, opens the folder, and takes out
a sheet of paper.

"Now," she says, "according to this, your Maths was
way above average for your age—outstanding even."

She glances up at me for a reaction.

"English good, too—neat, methodical, analytical
with a good imagination, it says here."

She leans back again and studies her pencil.

"I'm getting very different messages to that now,"
she says. "Mr. Henderson says he feels you'd be hap-
pier in another Maths set, where you could cope with
the work."

She gives me a long stare while I concentrate on the
tape holder on her desk.

"However, what really concerns me," she contin-
ues, "is that I understand your father died recently—in
a car accident, I believe?"

She looks at me like it's a question, so I give a nod.
She looks down at her pencil and starts to roll it again.

"How long ago was that, Joe?" she says, looking
up.

176

"I don't know. February—about seven months, I think."

"It can't be easy for you," she says, looking straight at me, "especially now—starting a new school, with new routines, new teachers, new classmates . . ."

I look out of the window, and she waits.

"What was he like?" she says after a long silence.

"Who?"

"Your dad—what was he like?"

"Just ordinary."

"Did he have any hobbies or interests?"

So I tell her about how he liked mending things, how they're still waiting on the shelf, how he used to go jogging every morning before breakfast. Then I remember these amazing sand castles he could build, like a towering helter-skelter, so that you could put a ball at the top and it would roll slowly all the way down and come shooting out through a tunnel at the bottom—how other kids would gather round and ask to have a go. How he was always losing his glasses—it drove Mum mad. How he hated milk . . .

I'm talking too much.

"You must miss him a lot," she says.

"Yeah."

"There's something else that concerns me too," she says, looking straight at me again. "I can't quite put my finger on it—but there's something unpleasant going on in this class. Is someone making things difficult for you, Joe?"

I study the tape again, and she leans forward.

"Is Alex Moss anything to do with it?" she says. "I shall find out eventually," she adds, giving her penetrating stare. "Look, perhaps I ought to write a note to your mother—ask her to come in so that we can discuss my concern. Would that help?"

Her eyes are on me again, as if she can read my mind. I stare at the tape.

"It is connected with Alex Moss," I say. "His dad was the driver of the other car—when my dad was killed."

It's not what she was expecting; I can tell by the way she's stopped rolling her pencil.

"I see . . ." she says after a bit. Then she starts flicking through another folder, frowning in concentration. "I was aware that Alex had problems at home—but not this. This puts an entirely different complexion on the matter. You should never have been put in the same class," she says, glancing up at me.

So I tell her how, like Richard said, it's all got out of control, about how the stuff that went missing wasn't Alex's fault, about the business in the changing rooms, about Dale's brother and the fight behind the trash cans and Alex's finger.

"This is very serious," she says when I've finished. "You realize that, don't you? If you had told me sooner it would have saved a great deal of trouble. Well, at least you've had the sense to tell me now. Come along—I think we had better go and find Mrs. Amos, Head of Year."

She stands and starts to gather up the folders, but first she takes out a letter and hands it to me. It's the one I faked from Mum, saying how sorry she was I'd been absent from school for two days with stomachache.

"Not unlike your handwriting, is it?" she says. "And did you know that stomach ends in ch, not ck?"

On the way home, after school, I make myself call by number thirty-six. There's no sign of A.M., but I reckon if he is pretending that he's setting off for school each day, he might still be here. I go round the side and, through the back door, I see him sitting at the table, reading, with a mug in his hand.

I knock on the glass. His head jerks in surprise. He stares at me, then returns to his reading. I knock again, but he ignores it. I turn the handle on the door, open it, and step in. He leaps up.

"Who do you think you are? Just get lost, will you?" he yells.

"I've got something to tell you."

179

"I don't want to hear it, right? Go on—bug off!"

"I've told Ms. Benton and Mrs. Amos . . ."

"You what?" And he starts toward me.

"Listen, I've told them about Dale and Stuart—everything. About Dale's brother, too—and about your finger. I said—I said it wasn't your fault! Right?"

He stops in front of me, fists clenched, like he's not sure whether to believe me or not.

"They rang my mum—she's got to go in tomorrow. They've probably rung your nan too—it is your nan you're living with, isn't it? Ms. Benton said. I'm just telling you so that you know—okay?"

He shoves his hands in his pockets and stands looking down at his feet.

"Why didn't you just leave it?" he says after a bit.

"I had to, didn't I? It wouldn't have stopped there, would it? Look—okay, blame me for starting it if you like. But I had nothing to do with the rest of it—the wallet in your bag, the socks down the bog, Dale's brother having a go. Yeah, I thought it served you right at the time. Especially after you grabbed me and cut off my tie and all the rest. . . ."

"So I was supposed to just lie down and let everyone walk all over me, was I?" he says.

"I'm just saying—none of that stuff came from me, right?"

180

"No," he mutters. "Just the poisoned chocolates and other nasty tricks."

"They weren't poisoned! You think I'm some sort of nut or something?"

He gives me a sideways questioning look.

"Yeah, well look—I thought you'd be pleased. You can't skive off forever."

"My nan's got enough on her plate without all this," he says. "Anyway, I'm leaving soon."

"Yeah, well . . ." I turn to go. "Was it that stuff I sent? Was that why your parents left?"

He starts to laugh, only it's not a real laugh.

"You really think a lot of yourself, don't you?" he says.

What's he talking about?

He sits down, stretches out his legs, and flicks a crumb across the table.

"You still think he did it, don't you? That it was his fault—that he got away with it?"

"No—I checked out what you said. I don't want to talk about it anymore."

"Oh, don't you?" he says. "Well, perhaps I do. You feel so sorry for yourself, don't you? Well, shall I tell you something? Sometimes—sometimes I wish it was *my* dad who'd been killed in that crash—not yours!"

"What?" I don't believe what I'm hearing; I know they didn't get on, but this is something different.

"Yeah—and shall I tell you why?"

He's looking straight at me now.

"Because it destroyed him. Because, even though it wasn't his fault, he couldn't forget he'd killed someone."

He starts to play with the bandage on his finger.

"At first it was just nightmares, but then he started to drink—to try and make himself sleep or forget, I suppose. But it didn't. He'd blame everyone else then—Mum mostly. Till nothing she did was right. If his dinner wasn't on the table the minute he came in he'd go mad. If he came home late he'd be yelling— why was it cold, or burnt or disgusting or something. I lost count of the number of plates he threw across the room."

He's not shouting now, just sitting there pulling a thread from his bandage and winding it around and around his finger.

"Oh, the next day he'd be sorry—please forgive me . . . how could I? . . . give me another chance . . . I don't know what got into me. Then he'd come home with some stupid thing he couldn't afford, like a microwave or a barbecue or a new bike, and Mum was supposed to be pleased. And the next night I'd be lying in bed hearing them shouting all over again. I'd lie there thinking, I wish it was him that was dead. Can you imagine that?"

He looks at me and then away again.

"Because at least I'd remember how he used to be. When I liked him."

His eyes are swimming, I can see, but he blinks them dry.

"How did you know it was me," I say after a bit, "that sent all that stuff?"

"I didn't at first," he says, "till I got to school and I learned who you were. Then I remembered—you used to deliver the papers, didn't you? But I'd seen you hanging around a few times, by the back gate. It just all fitted together."

"Are you going to tell them, then?"

"Why? Worried I might?"

"Only because of Mum—she's had a rough time. I'd rather she didn't know."

"Mum wanted to tell the police," he says, looking at me. "But Dad wouldn't. It was stupid—like he deserved it or something. You'd have been in serious trouble then, all right."

"Where have they gone, then?"

"They? You still don't get it, do you?"

He slides down in his chair and gives the leg of the table a kick.

"Mum couldn't take any more. She went to stay with my aunt in Hull for a break. She left me with Nan because she didn't want me to miss school. The next thing we hear is Dad's gone—no one knows where—and he's put the house up for sale. We haven't heard anything from him since. So Mum's going to get a job in Hull and get her own place, then I'll go up and join her."

He sits staring at his finger, then gets up, reaches for the juggling bags on the table, and starts to throw them.

"Doesn't your finger hurt?" I say.

"Not anymore."

"Did they break it, then?"

"What do you think?"

I watch him for a while.

"You're really good," I say.

He lets one of the bags drop onto his foot, then flicks it up, catches it, and the bags cascade over and over between his hands.

"Just practice and concentration," he says. "What's good about it is that you can't think of anything else while you're doing it."

"See you tomorrow, then," I say. "At school."

184

Chapter 20

Dale and Stuart have been separated and put in other classes. They were going to move me too, but after Mrs. Amos had seen Alex and me together, with my mum and his nan, they decided to leave it as it is. Dale's brother and his friend are in serious trouble; they've been harassing some of the year eights for lunch money as well, so that they have to spend all their break times in the Deputy Head's office and they're not allowed to leave school till ten minutes after the final bell.

"Why on earth didn't you tell me all this was going on?" says Mum as she drives us home afterward. "And is this Alex the same Alex that you said you were friends with? I don't understand, Joe." She's frowning at me. "Because if he is, then you were lying to me, Joe."

"I didn't lie, Mum. Not exactly. I said I saw a lot of him. I said we had a lot in common."

She pulls up at a traffic light and looks at me.

"I discovered where Long—I mean Terence Moss—lived. By accident really. So I started to watch the house, sort of spy on them."

Mum's staring hard at me, and I'm grateful when the light changes and we move off.

"It made me feel like I was doing something—for Dad—for you. That's where I kept going. I used to see Alex there sometimes. I'm sorry, Mum."

"Oh, Joe," she says.

"Mum—can you drop me off at Richard's?"

"Hello, Joe. Long time, no see," says Richard's mum.

"Richard! For you—it's Joe!" she calls up the stairs. "Come on in, Joe. How's your mum these days?"

"Okay, thanks."

I can see Richard halfway down the stairs, looking inscrutable. "Yeah, what?" he says.

"The perfect host," sighs Richard's mum. "Aren't you going to invite him upstairs, then, Richard?"

Richard turns and makes his way back up, and I follow him. He goes straight to his table and sits there, painting a figure with a tiny brush.

"Wow! You've got Lemmings," I say, peering down at his computer table. "And you've changed your room around."

186

"It's been like this for ages," he says with his back to me.

"Yeah, well . . ." I stand watching him, but it's like I'm invisible.

"What you doing?"

"I'm painting the Flesh-hound of Khorne's fangs red so it looks like blood. Next question."

I sit down on his bed.

"Would you rather be attacked by a Beast of Nurgle or a Horror of Tzeentch?" I say.

He puts his Flesh-hound down and turns round.

"Look, what is this about?" he says.

"You were right," I say. "It got out of control. They know all about it at school now. I told Ms. Benton and Mrs. Amos. I thought you'd like to know. Dale and Stuart are being moved into different classes. And I've talked to Alex. He's okay really, I suppose."

He stares at me. "So *that's* why you all disappeared during English," he says.

"Yeah—and my mum had to go, and Alex Moss's nan and Dale and Stuart's parents and Dale's brother and his friend Luke . . ."

"Hold on a bit," he's saying. "Dale's brother?"

So I tell him about the fight and Alex's finger and how he's living with his nan and grandad and why. And I tell him about how I knew who Alex was, about the spying. I don't tell him about the Nightmare Plan. As it is, it's like I'm talking about someone else, not me.

"So that's what you were doing in the holidays," he says.

"Yeah," I say. "I know it sounds crazy—even to me now. Anyway, I've got to go."

Later, as I'm watching *Knightmare,* the phone rings.

"It's not your turn," says Richard. "It's mine. Would you rather eat live cockroaches in strawberry sauce or a maggot sandwich?"

"I'll think about it," I say. "I'll let you know tomorrow."

Chapter 21

Alex's finger's okay now and things have more or less settled down at school, apart from some dirty looks from Dale and Stuart.

It's funny, what I said to Mum all that time ago, about me and Alex having a lot in common; it's true. The accident is part of both of us. It's like something we share. We don't talk about it, but it's there all the same. Mum made me invite him round for tea, and he's started to teach me how to juggle. It's not as easy as it looks, though. I can manage about twelve throws and then I lose the rhythm.

It's Saturday and we've arranged to meet at thirty-six, but he's not here, so I let myself in and start to practice over the bed; it's not so far to bend when you drop the bags.

Eighteen, nineteen, twenty . . . twenty-one! Twenty-one throws before a drop! A new world record for Joe

Harris! I hear Alex come in and I run down, yelling, "Just stand back and be amazed, then!"

He is amazed. Not Alex, but Longleat Man, who's standing in the kitchen.

"What the—?"

"Er—sorry. I thought you were Alex."

"Alex? Alex is here?"

"No—not yet. He said he'd meet me here—I'd better go."

"Don't I know you from somewhere?" he says.

"Yes—you might. I used to deliver papers here."

"When's he coming, then?" he says, looking around the kitchen.

I shrug. I've just noticed how many mugs and dirty plates and empty cans there are lying around; it looks like a tip.

"Seems as if he's been a regular little visitor," he says, gathering up some of the rubbish and chucking it into the bin. He starts to sniff the air, guided by his nose to the sink and the dishcloth. "Merry hell," he says, stepping back.

"Go on," he says, picking up the kettle, "sit down while you're waiting," and he starts to fill the kettle.

I try to tell him I won't stay, but he says, "Hold on a jiff," and disappears out the back door and comes back with a Sainsbury's bag and takes out tea and coffee and milk and a packet of chocolate cookies. He opens it and shoves them toward me. "Go on," he says, "help yourself."

"No, it's okay—I think I'd better . . ."

"Go on," he says as he makes the tea. "How many sugars?"

He sets the mug in front of me.

"Thanks."

"How is Alex, then?" he says, sitting down on the other side of the table. "I've been away a bit."

"He's okay."

I sip my tea.

"He's teaching me to juggle," I say for something to say.

"You both at the same school, then?"

"Yeah—we're in the same class."

"Is he still practicing his footwork?" he says.

"Yeah—he's really good. Mr. Gardener's always getting him to demonstrate."

"How about you?" he says.

"No—I'm barely average."

I cannot believe I'm sitting here, talking to him. He's not drunk; at least, I can't smell anything. He's not what I expected, and he's thinner too: his fat belly has gone. I concentrate on drinking my tea so I can go, but it's still a bit hot. He gets up, goes into the hall, and comes back with the big pile of envelopes and stuff and starts working his way through it on the table. I recognize one of the envelopes: a white one with my handwriting on the front. It's the last photo I took of his Escort after he'd sprayed over the scratch and the marker pen.

I swallow my tea. "I have to go now," I say. "Can you ask Alex to give me a ring?"

"Sure," he says, slitting open the white envelope. "Who shall I say?" he says, looking up.

"Joe."

"Right, Joe," he says. "Nice meeting you," and I see him take out the photo, stare at it, and turn it over. It's like I'm mesmerized, like a rabbit caught in headlights, and I can't move.

He sits down on a chair and puts the photo in front of him as if he's forgotten I'm here. And I hear my voice say, "I know who sent that."

"What?" He looks up, but I'm not sure he's really heard; he's thinking about something else.

"I know who sent the photo," I say, but I've got my hand on the doorknob, just in case.

He frowns at the photo, picks it up, and turns it over and looks at me again.

"I can tell you what it says on the back—'You can't cover up what you've done.'"

As he looks at me again the expression on his face changes, and I'm wondering if I should have kept my mouth shut. He's out of his chair now and he's bending down, holding my shoulders.

"Tell me, then!" he orders. "Because when I find him . . ."

He glares at me, then lets go, runs his hands over his head, and orders, "Sit down. Now, you'd better be telling me the truth," he says.

"It was me," I say. "And all the other stuff, too . . ." I give him the whole list.

When I've finished, he pulls his hand down over his face, like he's wiping something away, then he walks over to the window and turns his back to me.

"A kid," he's saying. "Just a kid . . . Why?" he says, turning to me. "Just tell me why?" He waits.

"It was my dad," I say. "It was my dad in the other car."

He stares at me like he's seen a ghost, then turns back to the window.

"Does Alex know about this?" he says after a while.

"He does now—but he didn't. There was a lot of trouble at school. I told people who he was—like, you know, that you were his father. He took a lot of stick.

I hated you and him. I was just so angry—especially after the court case. I couldn't take it—not that it was an accident. But then Alex said—"

"Alex?" he says, turning round. "What did Alex say?"

"He said it wasn't your fault."

He grips the back of a chair and leans on it.

"I'll pay for the damage—to the car. I've got some money saved up."

"What about Alex?" he says. "You said he was having a hard time. What's been going on?"

"Oh, stupid tricks—and there was a fight. His finger got broken. But it was sorted—it's okay now. Really."

He looks at me. "Your dad must have been one special person," he says.

I nod. I have to be careful or I'll blub again.

Then he gives a little laugh, more like a snort.

"A kid!" he says. "A bloody kid."

I leave, but I'm not sure if he notices.

As I pass the alley, Alex shoots out on his bike.

"Where have you been?" I say. "Your dad's there."

"You don't have to tell me—I saw his car," he says. "Why d'you think I've been hanging round outside?

You've been forever. What on earth have you been doing in there?"

"What—you knew? And you just let me come downstairs and find him there? You could have come in—I felt a total idiot."

He starts to pedal along slowly.

"I just didn't want to see him, that's all."

"He's got suitcases," I tell him. "I saw them on the backseat—I think he's come back."

There's no response from Alex.

"Listen, Alex—I told him. I told him it was me who sent all that stuff."

He stops. "You really are crazy," he says. "You know that?"

"I had to—I couldn't not."

He plays with his gears. "What did he do when you told him?"

"Nothing—he was a bit shocked like."

A.M. sits there, staring at the ground.

"He wasn't mad or anything. He wasn't like I expected at all," I say.

"Yeah, well—that's the problem, see," says Alex, not looking at me. "Some days he's okay. He fools you into thinking you might have imagined it all. Till the next day."

He fiddles with his gears, flicking the lever back and forth with his thumb. Then suddenly he pedals off, jerks the front wheel of his bike off the road, and glides along on the back wheel.

"Bet you can't do this," he yells.

"Yeah, but I haven't got some fancy ridgeback, have I?" I shout, catching up with him.

"Where are we going?" he says when we reach the end of the road.

"Have you heard the story of the woman with the haunted fridge?" I say.

"What?"

"Follow me!" I yell, pedaling off toward Vic's.

Chapter 22

It's nearly the end of the half-term break and I'm waiting on the steps of the Haymarket for Richard and the rest, but I'm early. Him, me, Simon, Jonathan, Rob, and Alex are going to Megazone. You have these laser guns and you run around trying to shoot one another without getting shot yourself, and at the end you get a scorecard. They say it's brilliant. Mum says I can bring them here for my birthday treat in a couple of weeks. She says it's a reward for doing well in Maths: I came fourth in the half-term test.

I can juggle three balls quite easily now, though Alex is on to four. He's back at thirty-six now; his mum moved back last week. He doesn't talk about it much, but it seems okay so far. He says his mum is giving his dad one more chance.

I wander over to the ice-cream kiosk and award myself a soft ice with chocolate sauce and nuts. Just in front of Littlewoods a man is drawing a picture on the pavement of Mary and baby Jesus. It's brilliant; just like something you'd see in an art gallery. The Christmas decorations are up already, and in the shop windows too. I still can't think about Christmas, though.

I sit myself down on the steps again, watching the people as they go past, the bright colors in the shop windows, the groups of kids hanging around Top Shop, and it's almost like I'm seeing it for the first time. It reminds me of those times when you go to the pictures and you sit in the dark watching *Arachnophobia* or something and you're seeing spiders everywhere and your skin's creeping. Then, when you come out, blinking into the daylight, you're amazed that the sun's shining, that people are walking about, by the absence of spiders, that the cars are going by. And you think, All this has been going on while I've been inside. Because while you're inside, it's like that's what's real. Well, that's how I feel now. I can't explain it any better than that.

Megazone was amazing, even though I got a rubbish score. It's already dark when I get home, though it's only half past five.

"Is that you, Joe?" calls Mum. "I'm upstairs."

I run up and see Mum's head poke round the bathroom door.

"What d'you think?" she asks, standing back.

The dingy gray wall has disappeared and she's using a wide brush to smooth out the creases of the wallpaper that now fills its place.

"Very nice," I say, though I still can't think why she wants all those flowers and butterflies.

"I quite enjoyed doing that," she says. "Not half as difficult as your dad made out. I've been thinking, we could do your room next."

"I'll think about it," I say.

"Well, you've changed your tune. I seem to remember you moaning regularly about its high embarrassment rating. Anyway," she says, gathering up all the scraps of paper from the floor, "I want it looking nice in time for Christmas. Auntie Jill and Uncle John and the twins are coming to stay. I thought that Kate could go in with Lucy, Ben could go in with you, and if I move in with Tom—"

"What? They're all coming for Christmas?"

"Yes—it's all arranged. I spoke to Jill on the phone this afternoon—and Gran and Grandad will be here too, of course. And on Boxing Day we're all going to the theater. Grandad's bought the tickets. He says it's his treat. What d'you think, Joe?"

"I think it's great!"

"We'll start on your room tomorrow, shall we?

We'll have to strip off that wallpaper first—then you can think about what you want on the walls. We could paint them if you like—any color you want."

"Yeah," I say. Dad won't mind. I know he won't.